So

A Typological Portrait of Solomon and the Shulamite Woman

by Mark Aho

Novel set by
Mark Meadows '
Solomons
Bride
..a tale of a king and a peasant girl.

The full Solomon's Bride Series:

Down from His Glory

The Shepherd King

The Stone and the Seal

Virgo Rising

The Bridegroom Cometh!

Available from
www.secretwineonline.com
www.amazon.com
www.bcfellowship.org

Solomon's Bride:
Down From His Glory

Published by Secret Wine

©2011

ISBN 978-1508540878

Cover design:
Mark Aho

Copyediting by The Final Touch Proofreading and Editing
www.finaltouchproofreadingandediting.com

All Bible quotations are from
the King James Version of the Bible

Secret Wine

Home of the World's Best Christian Reading

www.secretwineonline.com

Introduction to Solomon's Bride

By Lonnie Jenkins

Reading *Solomon's Bride* was for me an extremely unusual adventure, since I seldom take the time to read works of fiction. One of the secretaries in our office has been proofreading for the author, and she suggested I might enjoy the read. I took her up on it and found myself looking forward eagerly to each new addition to the series.

What a creative imagination Mark Aho has displayed to create *Solomon's Bride!* He has taken Bible characters and Bible events and filled in the blanks in a way only inspiration can accomplish. No attempt is made to depict this as a true story, just delightful and inspirational reading.

Inspirational? For you ladies, this is a beautiful love story. For the men, there are, oh so many scenes that hold Biblical and Message truths, for those who are included in the roll of members of the Bride of Christ. These lessons are woven in with such ease that unless you are well read in the Scriptures and are familiar with the teachings of William Branham, you will without doubt miss them. But to the student of these truths, the types speak so very loud and clear of the position the Bride has in relation to Christ; what he has done for us, provided for us, and expects us to act on. *My! Look what Jesus has done for me, and the confidence He has placed in me!* Sadly, we often do not... looking at all our own imperfections rather than what "He who knew no sin" has imputed to us.

In the portions where there is a display of the Biblically acclaimed wisdom of Solomon, Mark has had to have quite some inspirational wisdom himself to dream up the problem and then solve the issue … with beyond the norm in wisdom.

The types and shadows blended into the narrative are so many and so well done my desire was that not one reader would miss them. Thus I asked brother Mark if he could possibly do either an additional book or an appendix on *"Just In Case You Missed It,"* in which he explains what went on in this relationship between Solomon, (the Christ-type, as Son of David) and his sweetheart, Bride-to-be and ultimately Queen to the King, and how it applies to you, also. This book will bless you.

Lonnie Jenkins

Introduction to the 2nd Edition

When the *Solomon's Bride* series first released in 2011, I did not know what to expect. The response to my occasional comment that I was working on a book series ranged from curiosity, to excitement, to kind silence. That silence sometimes got even quieter if I explained a little more about the book's plan and thrust. But I am happy to report that the overwhelming majority of the feedback I have received from readers has been positive. The few—and I do mean few—who have given me other kinds of feedback, I have found generally fall into two categories: those who have questions about the books, and those who have read them. I have not yet received a single negative comment from any person from the second category.

Still the work is not without its faults, and bears the marks of a novice, being that it was my first attempt at writing on this scale. That has become more apparent to me as I have looked at it through the unforgiving lens of time, and my own skill in the craft has also improved in that time. There are many places where I think, *I could do that so much better now.* But, I suppose there could be no stretch of years in my writing life, when that would not later be the case. This is the private pain of any author, and I bear it alone. A complete re-write is impossible. Therefore, this edition has left most everything untouched, even that which curls my toes. As far as general style and content, the work remains as it was, with these comments added.

Through the Reader's Window

Different readers pick out different things, and sometimes, the odd detail is troubling to one person that everyone else reads over. This is particularly true when it comes to Bible subjects, for nothing else is a stronger magnet for strong opinions. I have encountered the occasional reader who reads along happily, until they find one thing that is at variance with their understanding of some Biblical point. If it is an important point to them, it can spoil the entire story, even if it is an unimportant point in the story. One Christian gentleman kindly informed me that Israelite kings never rode horses, only donkeys, and on that issue alone, he never read beyond the opening chapters. Whether that is historically true or not, it bears pointing out that the *Solomon's Bride* story is spiritual truth first, history second. Solomon as king is typing the King of Kings, and that king, we read in Rev. 19:11, comes riding on a *white horse.*

As an author I am disappointed when such things happen, feeling perhaps like a chef who has prepared a large banquet of various delights, only to finds the occasional person walking out because they don't like the seasoning in one particular dish. It is impossible for me to know exactly where every reader's hot buttons are, and if I attempted to steer around them all, there would surely be no story left. So, if this is your first time reading this story, I at the outset beg forgiveness for my ignorance on any such point you encounter, and ask if you will kindly spit out that bone and move on. There might be something ahead for you that you will really like.

The Endnotes

The main feature of this edition is the inclusion of endnotes, which explain certain Bible points that are made in the story. My Bible research while writing uncovered some possibilities that were surprising to me, such as Caleb being a Gentile, and Solomon, being the fourth born of David and Bathsheba rather than the firstborn, among other things. As the reader progresses through the books, it will be come apparent, I believe, that the points made are well researched. But since these surprising points are encountered early in the story, it is only fair to include, for the Biblically astute reader, the Biblical rationale for these proposals. Though they are not central to the story, they can still be a stumbling block for some readers. I offer the footnotes not to prove the points, but simply to demonstrate that the points were not made without due research and careful thought. Hopefully this will assist the reader to understand, even if he disagrees, that this is not a work of ignorance.

The Divine Literary Device

I occasionally hear the whisper, (if I am not imagining it) that reading fiction is "beneath" a mature Christian. Insofar as this admonishment is intended to steer its advisees away from non-edifying activities, (or just time wasting) I agree, and have little to do with fiction myself, as far as what the world calls fiction. But I believe it would be more becoming on a mature Christian to develop his understanding of literary categories from the Bible, rather than from how the world categorizes things. My former thinking has been corrected to understand that God, not man, invented the written word, and allowed it to be developed on earth for the specific purpose of being the carrier of His thoughts. It has no higher purpose, though it perhaps has a few mundane and practical purposes, such as for education, record keeping, and the various tasks of life. I think that much if not all of what is written outside of those purposes is a case of man hijacking God's instrument. Once man's dirty hands are on something, he adjusts and modifies it to suit his liking. Categories such as "fiction" and "non-fiction" and all the various subdivisions derive from man running away with God's horse. However, it is still God's horse, and He has never relinquished the right to use it for that which it was originally intended.

So the question is, what was that original intention?—how has God used the written word, in the past? We need not guess, the Bible shows us. If we form our understanding from what is modeled out in the Bible, we arrive at a set of categories different from the world, and these yield a very different result. In the Bible we find *history*, we find *poetry*, and we find *parable*, cast over a broad range of literary devices, including allegory, analogy, simile, and the like. The Bible uses this array of tools as vehicles to carry spiritual truth. *Solomon's Bride* makes use of the same. The story tends strongly to the parable side, partially to the history side, and occasionally to the poetry side.

So where is fiction in this list? When the Bible uses parable as a vehicle for spiritual truth, is it really "fiction" as the world calls it? Or is "fiction" merely the world's impersonation of "parable?" Parable, in the Bible, derives from the edification gift of teaching, and as the favorite teaching method of Jesus Christ, could lay claim to being God's *highest* vehicle for the placing of divine truth. (If the parables of Jesus Christ were published in a book and dropped off at a modern library for categorization, they would have no shelf to put them on but "fiction.") I would nudge the mature Christian reader to carefully ponder these points, and examine the categories that exist in his own mind and their origins, to be sure those origins are Biblical and not worldly. There just might be a pearl among the peas.

The Author Name

In this edition, I breathe a sigh of relief that I am using my own name, Mark Aho, rather than an author name, Mark Meadows. Though it is true that the meaning is the same, (my Finnish family name was not translated into English when my predecessors immigrated to America many years ago) the Anglicized version has never felt quite right to me. I am not known to my friends as Mark Meadows, but Mark Aho. At the time of first publishing, I was persuaded by the standard rationale to pick a name more palatable to an English speaking audience. After five years of that, I am still not comfortable with it. So, I am back as myself in this edition. In other editions, the pen name remains.

The Reading Audience

I did not have any particular audience in mind when drafting the story, but upon observation, I have found it has appealed almost evenly to men and women. I have occasionally been asked by parents if the *Solomon's Bride* series would be a good read for children, and at what age? Age twelve seems to be about the age children start reading the books on their own. Prior to age twelve, families have reported success in reading the story with and to their children, and for these families, it has sparked discussions with instructive and edifying value. The odd child may be able to approach the books at a younger age, but by observation, twelve seems to be the usual entry point. This is the same for both girls and boys, and the one exception that I know of who started younger, was a boy. To the parent who is considering this, I say, you know your own children. You read the books first, and decide for yourself.

Mark Aho, March, 2015

Author's Preface

When John Bunyan released *Pilgrim's Progress* in 1678, he inserted prior to the story a poem defending the type of book he had written. He called it "The Author's Apology for His Book." It is a long and clever argument in 235 lines. Still, Bunyan's book was criticized by many; its sin: the putting forth of spiritual truth in a format that had not at that time been seen before.

The author of *Solomon's Bride* is no John Bunyan, but upon learning of the struggle of Bunyan, realizes he may have created a book guilty of the same sin, for it also stretches the art to places unexplored. But what is unfamiliar is not for that reason invalid. So, lest the stones fly early, a few words of explanation are offered here to introduce the device this book uses, and what I hope to accomplish thereby.

The book you hold in your hands is what I call a "Typological Portrait." The author knows of no other example of this method. Those two words are carefully chosen: A *portrait*, not a photograph, because, unlike a photograph, which renders its subject exactly, a portrait takes a real subject and alters it to make an impression. It is the impression that is desired, not the exact rendering of the object. *Typological*, the modifying adjective is a word known to students of the Bible; it simply indicates one biblical event symbolizing in miniature another coming event— "type" and "anti-type." The bronze serpent on a staff which Moses held up in the wilderness for the healing of the plague (Numbers 21:4–9; John 3:14–15) is understood as a "type" of Christ on the cross for the healing of sin, thousands of years later—a divine wink, if you will, at something God planned to do in the future. If you are not familiar with this device, a reading of *Solomon's Bride* will hopefully serve as a good introduction.

As models for my portrait, I have chosen Solomon and the Shulamite woman. Others could have been selected—Boaz and Ruth or Isaac and Rebekah, for example, for they also supply the needed types. But the life of Solomon had aspects that allowed me to better present the truths at which I was aiming. Using these characters, I have imagined and dramatized them in their typological roles, rather than in their actual history. Solomon, the "anointed king" and "son of David," is understood as a "type" of the enthroned Christ, while his chosen bride is a "type" of His redeemed Church. It is the typological element rather than the history of these characters that drives the story.

Though imagination was harnessed to fill out this dramatization, the message of the dramatization is much more than imagination. The message was born of a good long soak in the Scriptures, absorbing their broad-sweeping themes, and then illuminating them in an artistic expression.

The entire Bible, Old and New Testament, is the lens that I have trained back upon the life of Solomon and of his queen, knowing that Solomon types Christ, as did his father David. This allowed me to pour back into their lives things that are not drawn from history. I neither claim nor intend to impart history in this story. History is already recorded; this story is fictional. What this story does is to take historical figures, Solomon and the Shulamite, and use them as props to illuminate the future, the coming kingdom of Christ and many other things. While the actual events in these novels are imagined, the anti-types to which they point are not.

Still, actual history has been utilized in the dramatization where possible. If the reader finds himself drawn to the Bible to learn whether Solomon actually said or did a particular thing, I consider that a healthy thing. However, it would disrupt the intent of this series of novels to stop and verify history at every point. The reader is encouraged, rather, to let the story flow along, and swim with its themes rather than being concerned about its details. Any reader who is searching for pure history is encouraged to search the Scriptures, not these books.

The historical Solomon is the subject of much criticism, and rightly so, for the sins of his old age are disastrous. The Scripture plainly says, "For it came to pass, when Solomon was old, that his wives turned away his heart after other gods: and his heart was not perfect with the LORD his God..." (1 Kings 11:4). I have noted carefully that the offense is applied to him "when he was old," *not* young. In the glory of his kingdom, Solomon is distinguished as the wisest man who ever lived. These facts combine to give us the most unlikely of character portraits: youth *and* wisdom. Most men, if they are foolish, are most so when they are young, but then grow wiser with age. For Solomon, it was the reverse. The fact that Solomon's heartbreaking end looms so prominently has perhaps spawned in Bible commentators a tendency to project the sins of his old age back upon his youth. This is unfair to the historical record and, if insisted upon, would surely destroy the intent of this novel set. Solomon's early years were glorious in every respect: youth, wisdom, riches, and righteousness. Fortunately for me, the whole of my drama takes place in this era, when his kingdom was at the zenith of its typological target: the millennial reign of Christ. I invite the reader to set aside for a time what is known of Solomon's end, and revel, as does this dramatization, is his glorious beginning.

The identity of the Shulamite woman is mysterious, and worthy of some discussion. In this story, the Shulamite woman is identified as Abishag, of I Kings 1. Though this remains a point of conjecture, there are good reasons to suspect that this was indeed she. Not the least among these is the fact that the words "Shunammite" of I Kings and "Shulamite" of Song of Solomon are essentially the same, the L and the N being interchangeable in the original language.[1] The town of Shunem, where most of this story takes place, is today called "Solam" which means "Peace." All the words: Shunem, Shulam, Solam, Solomon, Shulamite, and Shunammite are derivations of "shalom," meaning "peace." It is

---

[1] Unger, Merrill F. *Unger's Bible Handbook*. Chicago: Moody Press, 1966. 302. Also: Smith, William. L.L.D. "Shulamite, The" and "Shunem," *Bible Dictionary, Teacher's Edition*. Philadelphia: The John C. Winston Company, 1884 by Porter and Coates. 626.

the suspicion of this author that many plays on words take place in the Scriptures concerning these terms, which make for good poetry, but not always good clarity.[2] That Abishag was a most beautiful maiden, and also, a girl of the hill country, rather than the courts, also harmonizes well with the Shulamite woman of the Song of Solomon. This was enough to supply the woman for the "type" my story needed.

However... it could be not the case at all. Abishag is not expressly identified in the Scriptures as the same person as the Shulamite woman in the Song of Solomon. I encourage the reader to have the literary maturity to accept that, whoever the Shulamite was historically, she was *someone,* and as the chosen bride of the anointed king, she represents the Bride of Christ. I could find no better candidate for this than Abishag, and her unique position in the kingdom made for an interesting drama.

On the subject of drama, there are some points worth mentioning, for there is a fair bit of it in these books. Dramatization is not new to Christianity. Nor are allegory, parable, or many like devices. Preachers for centuries have used allegory as a tool to illustrate truth, often dramatizing Bible stories and characters. Jesus was famous for giving lessons in parables. It seems safe even to say that God Himself likes allegory, as it is used liberally in His own Scriptures. Therefore, it is in this spirit and this great tradition that I put forth this novel set. I submit that if the point of the allegory is in harmony with the plan and message of God as revealed in the Scriptures, it is more than permissible—it is helpful.

---

2 The Lamsa translation of the Peshitta Aramaic reads "Abishag, a Shilomite." I Kings 1:3. When this is compared to "Shulamite" in Song of Solomon 6:13, it will be noted that only the vowels differ. The King James renders the word "Shunammite," replacing the L consonant with an N. The word "shilomite" is also used by the Lamsa translation to refer to a later woman known to the prophet Elisha in II Kings 4:13, which is rendered by other translations as "Shunammite," meaning "a woman of Shunem." If in the view of one translator, the vowels are the same but the consonants differ, and in the view of another, the vowels differ but the consonants are the same, this suggests we are seeing nothing more than translator preference in how to render what is essentially the same word.

Doubtless this story has many faults, both in fact and in art. This is the natural product of an author who is replete with faults. I cannot write above what I am, and my many weaknesses certainly find their way into my story. But my desire to do something for the benefit of the Church—even poorly, if it were the best I could attain, relying upon the grace of the reader to make up the difference—was stronger in the end than the fear of failure. If the reader will have mercy upon me, this work will, I hope, even with its many faults, help in some small way.

Finally, I submit to you, dear reader, my sincere prayer that in all things you will be lifted up by this story, soaring on the winds of faith into a higher understanding of our glorious calling. I submit these tear-stained pages to you, as a gift to Him whom I am honored to call Bridegroom, in the hopes that, in blessing you, I can express my love for Him. I pray that He will receive my offering, and that you will be blessed.

Mark Aho

Dedication:

...To the Bride

and Bridegroom...

Come away with me, my love!
Come away to a land where colors can be smelled,
sounds tasted, and blossoming flowers make music.
A world beyond the mirror, where all is the same, yet all is different.
Enter now thy soul with reverence that secret place of hushed tones,
...of which the most fortunate have only heard second or third hand.
Cry all forever their unworthiness, any who catch a fleeting glimpse.
Shrink here to mere flecks, the grandest of thoughts of the wise.
Sleep boasts no dreams finer.
Fantasy blushes before reality.
Enter lucky soul!...enter and indwell!
That fragrance! Wild hopes fulfilled.
That glow! Amber rays,
flooding the soul with warmth.
If but once a man doth taste
a single drop of this honey,
he will gladly give his life
a thousand times
to find a second.
Divine . . .
Love.

Chapter 1

No creature has ever inspired more fascination in the sons of men than a troubled king.

What happened next was surreal. For Solomon, the mere fact that he was falling was not cause enough to concede impact with the bottom. After all, a lot could happen between now and then. He glimpsed the edge of the ridge from which his feet had separated, while his hands flailed for a bush and missed. So many things cease to matter in a freefall. It is amazing how many thoughts can flash through the mind in a blink of time. Amazing that thought is possible at all when the body is in mortal peril. And the insights—so profound! But why? Why such pearls of perception when there remains so little time to appreciate them?

No matter—save that question for another time; the more pressing issue must be addressed: somewhere between here and impact with the rocks below, he must devise a clever solution to the suddenly inconvenient law of gravity. Panic clawed at him.

Will they call it a suicide?

He swatted at the thought like an insect.

No. Absolutely not. Not now, not like this.

"They'll say its her fault—she drove him to it..."

Silence!

The wind rushed by his ears and beard as he gained speed. He curled and tried to right himself, but the tall angular body of King Solomon, though graceful, was not suited to such acrobatics. The rough hyssop brush of the hill country blurred past his vision in the dusky evening light. White limestone rocks and boulders streaked by. Scarcely an instant had passed.

I will solve this...

He reached for his gift of wisdom as for a trusted sword, but was interrupted by the rocky slope contacting his shoulder. The world went tumbling—earth, sky, earth, sky—

Wisdom! Where art thou?!

Then . . . time . . . froze. The present faded into mist, and a new scene flooded his vision, invading without invitation, like a pulled screen.

Am I dead?

A room opened before him. He recognized the scene! Suddenly, he was no longer a depressed twenty-two-year-old king in the sixth year of his reign, alone in a strange wilderness, rapidly descending toward an uncertain fate. He was in the past.

I have heard of such things—the flashing of life before the eyes of a soul facing imminent death.

He was floating near the ceiling, gazing down upon a happy scene: a carefree eight-year-old boy engaged in play with a friend on the floor of his father's palace. The boy was himself, and the playmate was a girl named Chavah. The melodious tones of his father David's voice wafted up, as he conversed with his guest and friend, Chimham. In the corner sat Solomon's mother, Bathsheba, and her maid. He remembered the day clearly...

The boy glanced up at Chavah. What was life without Chavah? What was the world without Chavah? Chavah was always there. She was as much part of the palace where Solomon was raised as the potted palms that bordered the cool stone steps.

The little blond curl, which often escaped from Chavah's head scarf, was dangling under her chin like a silent bell. Her eyes remained fixed on the tiny carved toy soldiers Solomon was arranging before her. It was a boy's game—an imaginary army defeating an imaginary enemy—but Chavah enjoyed it just the same. As young Solomon narrated it to her, her eyes wandered to and fro. Chavah enjoyed all of Solomon's games, and Solomon loved her.

From the perch of his vision, the full grown Solomon looked down upon his father, watching as King David leaned back and laced his fingers behind his head. Solomon knew these were good days for the king of Israel. Most of his troublesome enemies had been pushed back, and for the first time in his tumultuous life, his kingdom was enjoying a measure of security. Even his adultery with Bathsheba, which had marked the darkest hour of his life, had been purged by the God of Israel in a surprising display of grace. The son of David's sin had died, but after David finished mourning, there came a new and surely undeserved gift: Bathsheba became David's legal wife, and three sons were born to them. Then came the fourth: Solomon,[1] an exceptional boy, too excellent in mind and heart to be anything less than a divine gift—proof that God had buried David's sin in the sea of grace.

David glanced around, drinking in the sweet domestic music of the scene around him: the children playing cheerfully, the women chatting pleasantly in the corner, the warm evening air of summer playing with the drapes as it entered the dining chamber to refresh the occupants. His loyal friend, Chimham, a frequent guest at his table, was at his side. Chimham's presence in the royal court was a constant reminder to David of his victorious return to the throne in Jerusalem, for it had been Chimham's father Barzillai who had escorted him safely back through the territories of his enemies. In repayment, Chimham was given a place at the king's table—for life. Whenever together, David felt blessed, and Chimham grateful.

Chimham's voice sounded unexpectedly.

3

"I have a request to make of you, my king, if I have found any favor in your sight."

David turned to Chimham, seeing on his friend's face an expression both peculiar and intense.

David placed his hand on Chimham's shoulder.

"If you have found any favor in my sight? Come now, brother, we are certainly beyond such as that. What is it that you require? Just speak it."

"Did you not promise to my father, Barzillai, that whatever I asked of you, you would give to me because of my father's kindness to you?"

"As you have spoken it, so it is, and your wish is my thanks. What do you ask of me?"

"Only this," Chimham replied, motioning to the floor. "Your son, Solomon, and Chavah, my daughter: see them, how they thrive together in your royal court? Though they are but children, their hearts are as one. I am indebted to your kindness on behalf of my father, and I know that as long as I live, you will be kind to me. But, look, I have no sons to carry my name forth—only my daughter, Chavah. How shall I know, when you and I have gone the way of all the earth, that my daughter will enjoy the same favor with your successor as I do with you? Therefore, promise me this: that my daughter, Chavah, will be the wife of your son Solomon, for your servant knows that you have already intended that Solomon will be king after you."

David's eyebrows arched in surprise.

"I have declared no such thing! How is it that you have come to know what is in my mind?"

Chimham shrugged.

"Is it not the duty of a servant to know the mind of his king? For, in so doing, I can serve you the better. However, be you assured that I dare not declare your secret to others. Certainly, that honor is for the king alone."

David looked upon his friend fondly. Seeing his son Solomon

and Chavah playing amiably on the floor in front of him, he could think of no good reason why the request should not be granted.

"I gladly give you your request," David declared and looked about for a servant. Seeing one by the door, he motioned for him to come. "Chimham and I have agreed to cut a covenant. Please, go prepare the animal and bring Zadok, the priest, here as witness."

At that, Bathsheba and her maid looked up, perceiving that the tone of the conversation had changed. David motioned for them to come forward.

"I have an announcement to make," he declared. Then he turned and addressed Chimham.

"I have not forgotten the kindness of your father, nor my promise to you on his behalf. What you have asked for, I grant you this day, for your daughter Chavah is a worthy girl, just as you are a worthy man, and she will be the wife of my son Solomon all the days of her life."

Bathsheba and her maid duly gushed at the unexpected development.

Chavah did not notice the conversation, but the sense of it was caught by the always alert young Solomon, and he looked up. The words of David, *she will be the wife of my son Solomon all the days of her life,* inflection and all, were in a moment permanently etched upon his bright young mind. In later years, others would remind him of the vow, but he needed no reminder; he had heard it for himself. And now, through vision, he was hearing the same fateful words again, as he watched the scene unfold.

The boy Solomon returned to the game on the floor. He had just gotten to the point where the king returns victorious from battle.

"And then what happens?" Chavah asked, fully caught up in the imaginary game.

"Then the king marries his queen, and they live together in the palace forever."

5

Chavah liked that. The mention of a queen sparked her imagination anew. She pursed her lips in an expression both familiar and endearing. She shook her head and blinked, her blond curl swinging, and then the smile burst forth.

"Queen!" she exclaimed. "Tell me about the queen! What is she like?"

"The queen? Oh, the queen is the loveliest person in all the palace," Solomon replied. "The king loves her and takes care of her and gives her whatever her heart desires. All the people of the city admire her."

Chavah's eyes traveled up toward the ceiling in private vision. She looked back over at her playmate. "Do . . . do you think I could become a queen one day?"

"You don't become a queen, a person must be born one," Solomon replied, "like you."

Chavah beamed.

Solomon, tossed a glance at his father and added, "And I will be your king."

"But I don't know how to be a queen."

"I will show you how. Tomorrow we can play a new game. We'll play *King and Queen.*"

"King and Queen! Yes—tomorrow. Can we? Is it truly a wonderful game?"

The boy Solomon looked into her wide sparkling eyes. He had just invented the game, but Chavah was such an agreeable spirit that he was confident anything he tried with her would work.

"It is the best of all games."

The scene faded to gray, and the room disappeared before the invisible onlooker. Suddenly, new images flooded his vision, like breaking clouds. He was now outside the palace. The scene which opened before him tugged deeply at his emotional memory.

Young Solomon and Chavah were skipping out into the

garden yard. It did not take the children long to invent many variations of *King and Queen*. They would play it while running through the courts, hiding behind pillars, skipping around the knees of nervous palace guards. Solomon remembered all of this. But the final scene made him wince in melancholy reminiscence.

Young Solomon and Chavah settled on an area in the garden as their favorite place to play *King and Queen*. Solomon named various plants and bushes to be imaginary palace guards and other characters in his never-ending story, and eventually transformed the whole garden into a make-believe city. In a place by the fishpond where the grass grew lush and green and the warm sun played upon the water, Chavah and Solomon were in their "palace." They would spend long hours together, never tiring of each other's company, as the warm light lingered long into the savory summer evenings.

He saw his mother Bathsheba approaching. Bathsheba, noticing the rooms of the palace growing still and quiet late in the day, would go out and look for the children. There she would often find them, asleep on the grass, Chavah curled up on Solomon's shoulder. Solomon saw his mother and her maid come with servants, take up the children, and carry them, asleep, back into the palace.

Then, he was falling again.

Chapter 2

In a blink, reality replaced the vision. King Solomon's desperate fall from the ridge had progressed not an inch from where he had been when the vision first overtook him. Time had halted while he was away. Awareness of the present now rushed back upon him. He had been hiking in the wilderness and tripped near a ridge, and was falling—still. Now he caught a fleeting glimpse of the shadowy bottom rushing quickly up from below. In a mental reflex, he reached again for his gift of wisdom, but before it could be grasped, the present escaped again, as a bird from the fowler, and another vision flooded in.

He found himself floating above the crowded assembly hall of David's palace. A young boy was craning his neck to see over taller people standing in front of him. The boy could only achieve a partial view of the drama in the royal court, but his intrigue was genuine, and he was more sharply attentive than anyone guessed.

"Will none dare to accept our challenge?"

The crier's voice echoed in the royal court, the stone walls reverberating until the sound faded into a cool silence. The crier and his master had been given entrance to the royal palace to present an evening of entertainment. They offered a bag of jewels to anyone who could best their champion in a battle of wits.

"A jewel for us if we win; the whole bag for you if you win," the crier added, searching the room with challenging eyes.

King David and the royal court were amused by these colorful Arabians. Win or lose, they brought drama to the court, presented themselves with flair, and promised an evening of first-class entertainment. They were professional performers, clever and convincing, offering a rich reward to anyone who could defeat them. The wisest men in many great kingdoms had already fallen before their challenge. Their champion, Alakhi Benishish, a figure imposing in confidence, sat before a gaming board topped with strange carved pieces of white and black arranged on marble and ebony squares.

Joab, the Israelite general, had tried first—not that he considered himself wise, but he was by nature a battler and did not want to be found shrinking from any challenge. Alakhi Benishish had finished him off quickly, and Joab good-naturedly dropped a jewel into the bag of his vanquisher.

"And it is published that Israel is haunted with wise men as numerous as the jewels of Ophir!" the crier called in exaggerated surprise. "Never before have I encountered a report so at odds with the reality!"

The room was tensely quiet as the attentive occupants watched nervously to see who would step up next. Quiet urges and friendly ribbing passed among the attendees. Many wanted to try, but realized their chances of beating the master at his own game were slim.

The torches grasping the high stone walls cast curious shadows over an array of amused and pensive faces. Visibly stationed were the high princes: Adonijah, Amnon, Absalom. Beautiful. Proud. Superbly attired. Glowing like ornaments in their customary place to the right of the king. King David looked over at his sons, who exchanged amused glances with him and one another, but moved not.

"Oh, King David!" the crier called out. "The valiance of your underlings shamefully fails them! Are we forced to conclude that there is but one wise man in all of Israel, and he has already fallen? Have you not another? The kings of Midian produced for us no less than twelve men of wisdom who vexed us for four and twenty hours!"

David was smiling.

Suddenly, there was rustling at the back of the room. Heads turned toward the noise.

"The prophet Nathan," someone whispered.

The crowd parted, revealing a plainly dressed, rugged old man with a staff. Nathan stood before the court. The attention of all was fixed upon the prophet, for wherever the prophet walked, drama followed.

Alakhi Benishish and the crier exchanged a glance and studied the strange-looking old man.

"Is this . . . the wisest in all of Israel?" the crier asked.

Nathan offered no response. The crier glanced at his partner, then back at Nathan.

"Let him come forth and display his wit!"

Silently, Nathan shuffled forth to stand before the crier, not uttering a word. After a moment of curious examination passed between the gamesman and the prophet, the crier asked, "Were you here to learn the rules?"

"I have not come to play," Nathan said, shifting his gaze to the gamesman from the crier.

Murmurings echoed in the room.

"For I am not the wisest in all of Israel," he added.

The gamesman cocked his head curiously. The observers rustled.

"However," Nathan continued, "the wisest is in this room tonight."

The room's occupants exchanged curious glances. The high

11

princes hesitated to take their eyes off the old prophet for even an instant, apprehensive that he might call on one of them.

"Is he then going to come forth?" exclaimed the crier in an exaggerated voice.

Nathan stared at him a moment, then turned away. Solemnly, he moved, the crowd parting before him like falling stands of wheat, until he came to the back of the room and stood before the youth who had been so attentive from the beginning—a slender twelve-year-old boy with wavy black hair and dark eyes. Every gaze followed. The prophet approached, and stopped, right before the boy. The eyes of the boy grew wide. Nathan extended his hand.

"Come, son."

Adonijah stifled a laugh and looked at his brothers. The boy Solomon blushed, his ears burning red with embarrassment. He took the hand of the prophet and was led past his two living older brothers, Shobab and Nathan, past Joab, Benaiah, and the chiefs of David's mighty men, past the skeptical eyes of the high princes, dignitaries, elegant queens, David's wisest men and advisors, and was brought to stand in front of Alakhi Benishish, the master of the strange game of wit.

The gamesman looked amused.

"Am I to understand that *this* is the wisest in Israel?" he asked.

"No."

The gamesman stared at the prophet blankly.

"Before you stands the wisest . . . in the world."

Audible gasps were heard. If the declaration had come from any but the prophet, they would have been laughs.

The old gamesman, not familiar with the prophet, was in truth amused. The old man studied the boy curiously, then glanced back at the prophet, a trace of a smile on his savvy old face. He flicked his eyes over toward his crier and back. The crier winked.

12

"Indeed?" said the gamesman. "Have you a jewel, my boy?"

Suddenly, the voice of David was heard.

"He does."

Heads whipped around to behold King David, descending from his place of honor to draw near and put his arm around the boy.

"Take courage, son," he whispered. "I know what it is like to stand before a giant. Remember who called you here, and do your best."

He placed a jewel on the table next to the gaming board.

"Very well," said Alakhi Benishish. "As I explained to my last opponent, the pieces move in this fashion…"

"I understand the game," the young Solomon cut him off.

The gamesman looked up curiously.

"From back there?"

Solomon blushed, and nodded yes.

"Well, then," said the master. "Nothing hinders that we may begin—but you understand that an illegal move results in a loss."

Solomon nodded.

The gamesman positioned himself behind the board, glanced up at his young opponent and back at the game, then ceremoniously moved a piece to the center. Solomon reached out with a slender white hand and replied.

After several moves, it was evident to Alakhi Benishish and everyone in the room that the young Solomon had indeed caught the sense of the game, even from the back of the room where he had deliberately hidden himself, as was his habit. After several more silent moves, Solomon suddenly gasped in self-disgust. After three more moves, it was over.

"That was well done, son," Alakhi Benishish said, taking the jewel into his bag. "For a first time, that was perhaps the best I have seen."

13

Solomon was not looking at Alakhi Benishish. He did not seem to hear him at all. His eyes were fixed on the board, darting back and forth vigorously. The gamesman was waiting for some courtesy from the boy, and looked around curiously.

"Again," Solomon whispered.

The room rustled.

Alakhi Benishish looked up peculiarly, and over at the crier. The crier looked over at the king. David descended to the center once again.

"Very well," he said with an odd smile. "One more jewel."

He placed it next to the board and returned to his seat.

Alakhi Benishish reached out and ceremoniously opened exactly as he had in the prior game.

The young Solomon stared at the gaming board. Time passed in silence. He continued to stare. The sights and sounds around him faded away like a dream while the game before him became the whole world. He placed both his hands on the sides of his head and leaned forward. He felt his consciousness changing as though he were descending into a tunnel. There was a flow around him . . . first a trickle, growing to a stream, then a torrent—a flood of minutia coursing through and around his awareness, his thoughts speeding forth, darting and dancing over the patchwork before him—chain upon chain upon chain. The room grew tensely quiet.

After several long minutes, the slender white hand rose again and placed a piece, differently than before. Alakhi Benishish did not respond instantly this time. After a moment of thought, the master moved again. Solomon again remained still for several tense minutes before moving another piece. The master paused once more, longer this time. So it went: Solomon carefully considering, Alakhi Benishish taking more time for each reply, the curious glances cast at his young opponent gradually giving way to more urgent ones. As the game wore on, the old master of the game of wit began exceeding the young Solomon in the time he took to consider his moves. Pieces danced and shuffled on the gaming board, and trades ensued. The crier was scowling at the board and at the lad, glancing nervously at the bag of jewels.

One by one, the game pieces left the board and took up new positions alongside it. After nearly an hour of tense silence, only a fraction of the original objects remained, and the breathless crowd had crept forward in silent attention.

"That will be all," Alakhi Benishish whispered, after a complicated exchange that left hardly anything on the board.

"What happened?" David asked.

"There is no longer enough material for a victory. The game is a tie," he explained. David looked around. The crowd whispered one to another.

"What happens now?" David asked.

"A third game," Solomon replied. His eyes remained locked onto the board, as if nothing else in the world existed.

The old master wiped sweat from his forehead. The crier looked nervously at the bag of jewels, then over at Alakhi Benishish. The Arabian partners exchanged an eloquent glance.

"The great Alakhi Benishish maintains a two-game limit for any single opponent!" the crier suddenly declared.

The assembly moaned loudly in disappointment. Voices began to chorus in protest.

"Of course he does," the casual voice of David cut into the room, causing the protests to fall silent, as he walked down to place his hands on the shoulders of the young Solomon. He stood before the gaming team, a twinkle in his eye.

"Of course, the great Alakhi Benishish has a two-game limit. He is an old man, and Solomon young and strong. An old man can not be expected to continue such strenuous concentration as long as this tender youth. But the court of Israel does thank you for a night of fine entertainment," he said to them with a smile.

David picked up the jewel he had placed beside the board and dropped it in the bag.

"For your kindness in showing us what indeed dwells among us," he explained. "You may return and try again at a time of your own choosing.

"Come, son," he said to Solomon, patting him on the shoulder. "I have a jewel for you also."

The Arabian gaming team looked relieved. The audience looked amazed. Adonijah and the other high princes looked sullen. And the entourage of gaming Arabians never again returned to cast their challenge before the courts of Israel.

The scene faded to black, and instantly, Solomon was back in his desperate plunge, his mind quick enough to calculate in a flash that he had descended several cubits during the last vision. He would impact the bottom in under a second! But again, before he could act, the present escaped, and he found himself gazing out from a parapet, the city of Pharaoh spreading before him. He was in Egypt, a young prince on an educational journey—part of his training to take the throne of Israel.

Chapter 3

In my years in the palace, visitors who observed King Solomon from a distance would sometimes query me concerning the grandeur of his kingdom, the elegance of his possessions, the depth of his wisdom, the weight of his gold. To all such questions I had one reply: The Solomon I knew was veiled by the glare of his wealth. Hidden behind his outward adornments was a man of such obsessive compassion, that he once ordered an entire royal caravan to pause in the road so he could lighten a peasant girl's burdens by showing her how she could better balance her load.

—Reflections of the Shulamite

Young Solomon, fourteen and tall, gazed out over the parapet, the city of Pharaoh stretching dazzlingly before him. Yet his eyes were unseeing. The depths of the naiveté of Chavah, his presumptive queen-to-be, had become painfully apparent in this far-away land, much more than among the friendly and forgiving residents of the royal house in Jerusalem.

Is she truly that unaware?

Time and again the question haunted him as he observed her behavior among the young men of other lands. Chavah, to be charitable, was innocent, perhaps even sheltered. But when among new acquaintances, it did seem that she enjoyed the lavish attention more than necessary, especially attentions from those who, it was clear to Solomon, had more than just a friendly interest in the sparkling young Israelite princess.

He tried to imagine defenses for her behavior.

She was raised without a mother to train her.

Unfortunately, his gift of wisdom was not so easily persuaded. His own mother, Bathsheba, had invested a great deal of time and effort into Chavah.

To be honest, her challenge was perhaps greater than that of other young maidens; she was queen apparent, for one thing, a fact which always attracted attention. But beyond that, she possessed a personality that won her quick favor in any group. She was witty, articulate, entertaining, bubbling, infectious, talented—these all were words whispered among those newly introduced to her. She was not long in any social setting without soon finding herself the center of attention. And from her perspective, what was wrong with that? She was doing no harm— simply spreading joy and happiness around.

Still, he thought, *there ought to come a time for her to pull away from the crowds, and let her loyalty to me be seen publicly.*

Solomon had found such occasions few, to be kind, and missing altogether, to be honest. Moments before, Chavah had just bustled by, alongside a dazzling young Egyptian prince. The pair had been seen together quite regularly over the past several days. And so the young Solomon stood alone, looking out over the city.

"With what lofty matters is the future king at this moment so occupied?"

Solomon lurched in surprise at the sound of a mature and dignified voice and turned to see Naamah, the Ammonite princess, who had come up behind him unnoticed. She stood dark, silent, and motionless, her deep eyes regarding him with patient stillness, allowing her question to hang in the air, her eyes not moving from him.

"You speak Hebrew," Solomon observed.

"Yes."

"You are not Egyptian," he noted.

"No."

Naamah returned Solomon's gaze with still confidence, apparently unafraid of prolonged silence.

"You are observant for an Israelite."

Solomon's eyebrows went up in surprise.

"What did you say?"

Naamah tilted her head to the side slightly and shrugged one shoulder, a thin trace of a smile touching her full Arab lips.

"I am an Ammonitess; I have lived among Israelites my entire life. And I have noticed a distinct lack of curiosity among your people."

Solomon smiled.

"You are observant—for an Ammonitess."

Naamah merely nodded slowly and smiled back with her eyes.

Solomon explained, "My parents are Israelite, but I have been raised to understand the world beyond just Israel."

Naamah nodded again.

"So how is it that the future king of Israel can be exposed to such pollution, when its people can not?"

Solomon chuckled at the princess's forthrightness. Taking a friendly tone, he explained.

"Your candor is refreshing, and your question is fair. You desire to reconcile your understanding that we Israelites do not mix with foreigners, with the fact that I am educated in their ways. Your understanding is accurate but incomplete. Since you know my tongue, perhaps you know something of my God as well. The history of my nation reveals a God who chooses whom He will. Though as sons of Jacob, we are carriers of a unique promise, there is no lack of examples of our God choosing non-Israelites for important works. Israelites are not His only interest, for He is the God of all. His children are everywhere. Perhaps you have heard of the great warrior, Caleb. He was not an Israelite.[2] As the future king, I represent the God of Israel, not because I am Israelite, but because God has chosen me, just as He chose my father's great-grandmother, Ruth . . ." Solomon paused for effect, "the Moabitess."

Now it was Naamah's turn to be surprised. In characteristic fashion, Solomon had turned the irony back on his conversation partner. Naamah showed her surprise with quiet dignity, cocking her head slightly to one side while a single eyebrow rose.

"Moabite," she repeated thoughtfully. "You are aware that Moab is a sister nation to Ammon; both Moab and Ammon were descendants of Lot."

"Yes, I know."

"So, if your God could choose for His servant a Moabite wife, certainly an Ammonite wife would not be out of the question."

Solomon opened his mouth, then hesitated. She had deftly met his irony and upped it with a clever counter of her own. From whence did this girl come, suddenly emerging from the shadows as she had to entice him into an interesting conversation?—if you could call her a girl, for she was suddenly sounding and looking very much like a woman.

"Your tongue is adventurous, Ammonitess."

"So I have been told. My father says I was born with a tongue of salt. He beats me, because he can not answer me."

Solomon blew out a chuckle that was part amusement, part curiosity.

"Truly? And what do you tell him that he can not answer?"

"I tell him that men and women are equal."

Solomon felt his lips stretching into a slight smile.

"On what do you base this . . . conclusion?"

"I contend that a woman, given the same opportunity, can

equal a man in any endeavor, and surpass him in many."

"True enough," Solomon said, nodding as if in thought.

For the first time the Ammonitess's eyes brightened just a touch. She carefully examined his face. She had thus far not found a man capable of admitting what she had just heard him confess.

"You agree with me!"

"Indeed."

She stared at him as if she had just discovered the lost treasures of Amenhotep.

"So why then are not men and women regarded equally?!"

"Because they are not equal."

The words hit her like a brick. She blinked.

"Not eq—?! How can you reconcile that with what you have just admitted?"

He looked at her kindly, noticed the red tinge behind her dark complexion, and took a gentle tone.

"I would call to witness the whole world, my Ammonitess friend. It is no less than the sum of all of its inhabitants. If men and women were equal in all *ways* . . ."—he paused for effect—"they would be equal in all *things*," he concluded, letting his palms open in a shrug.

Her mouth dropped open and she inhaled as if to say something, but hesitated, her salty tongue finding no instant reply.

"Add to that the puzzling question of why one exact equal would be in need of special treatment from another," he added, preempting the reply she was just beginning to locate.

She glared at him for several pensive moments, then huffed and looked away sharply. He waited. Turning back to him, she declared, "I can not accept that women are inferior," fire burning deeply in her eyes.

"Inferior? Unequal and inferior are two different things, friend. Is the moon inferior to the sun? In brightness, yes, but in beauty, no. Is the river inferior to the sea? In size, yes, but in speed, no. Such things are unequal, but neither is inferior, and I, for one, am glad for it. Are not some inequalities required to form harmonies? Without harmonies, the world would have no music. So it is with men and women, if they were equal, it would spoil the song."

She was eyeing him suspiciously. He tossed her a wink.

"But in the case of you and your father, if you were considered equals, I suspect the compliment would be more his than yours," he added.

She blinked as the clever flattery in the comment found its target. If a rebuttal was in order, it was now time to speak it, but Naamah was suddenly not sure if his comments truly insulted her gender. Her adventurous tongue remained restless but silent, unable to find a barb that would penetrate his surprising volley— if there were a deserving target for one to hit, and of that she was suddenly not sure. How had he so quickly scattered her arguments on her favorite topic into such a puzzling array of ambiguities? She did not know, but of this she was quickly becoming aware: the young Israelite king-to-be was not the ignorant pampered child of privilege she had assumed. He was dangerously clever, but tempered it with a disarming kindness and displayed none of the acidity that she had come to expect from men when forced to address the current subject.

Solomon regarded with curious intrigue the bold young Ammonitess who stood before him with her shiny black Arab hair and dark, intelligent eyes. She was manifestly clever of mind, but misinformed, especially about the God of Israel, which was a topic more interesting to him than the last. Their short conversation had already proven her a worthwhile conversationalist.

"Naamah." Solomon spoke her name for the first time, revealing that he did remember it, though they had not been officially introduced. Her head snapped up at the sound of her name.

"You have implied something about our God. Could one of

our people take an Ammonite wife, as my father's great-grandfather married Ruth? This is a fair question. Our God is not exclusive, as you perhaps suppose. He is sovereign, something different entirely. He chooses whom He wishes, and if He approves, who can resist His will? But in your case, the objection would come from your god. I don't think Milchom would approve."

At the mention of the Ammonite deity, Naamah stiffened, a cloud of fear passing briefly over her face. She recovered quickly.

"I was not asking to be *your* wife. My place in my own kingdom is not in doubt, I assure you."

"I doubt not your place. It is your kingdom that gives me pause for question," Solomon said.

Naamah did not have an instant response to that.

He added, "Besides that, I have already been promised a wife."

"So I see. Is her behavior typical of Israelite wives?" she asked, indicating with a tilt of her head the direction in which Chavah had recently walked.

The backs of Solomon's ears suddenly felt hot.

Turnabout is fair play.

He had no graceful answer to her astute and well-put question.

Naamah rescued him from the uncomfortable moment by gracefully moving from the position where she had been standing to lean on the rail next to him, casting her gaze out over the city.

"Why do you doubt my kingdom?"

"My father wears its crown," he replied. "Why do you doubt my wife?"

"Isn't it obvious?"

She looked knowingly into Solomon's face. It was impossible for him to hide his blush, and he discerned that to attempt an explanation would only worsen his state. He was suddenly wary of

23

her; their short conversation had already revealed that she possessed a clever intellect. He also noticed that she had an exotic kind of beauty and seemed older than her years.

"Let me tell you something about my kingdom that you may not know," Naamah offered suddenly, casting her dark eyes back out over the sparkling city, her long, black hair swinging from the quick movement. "The throne and the crown of Ammon do not belong to the king of Ammon; they belong to our god, Milchom. Sometimes there is a man to represent him on the earth; other times, as is the case now, there is not. In either case, my place in his kingdom is secure, for I am betrothed either to the king, if he lives, or to Milchom himself in the eternal kingdom. If I do not marry the one, I will marry the other, which would be superior by far."

Solomon chuckled. "And just how do you propose to marry Milchom?"

Her expression grew grave, accompanied by an unexpected silence.

"There is a ceremony . . . on the morning of the Spring Equinox of my eighteenth year, at first light . . ."

The shocking realization descended upon Solomon like a dark cloud. Human sacrifice being entirely foreign in Israel, he had not been thinking along such lines at all. He paused for a moment, trying to discern how one might be expected to respond to such a revelation. Were congratulations or apologies in order?

"Is there any means by which you might avoid this . . . wedding?"

"There are two ways. I could be disqualified if I were found to not be a virgin."

"And then?"

"I would be immediately burned alive with fire, and in the afterlife, I would be the object of Milchom's eternal rage, rather than his wife."

"What is the other way?"

24

"As I said, I could be married to the earthly king of Ammon."

"But Ammon has no king."

"I see," she responded in a tone that showed her mind had lit upon an irony. "Well, I am afraid I must disagree with you, Israelite, and I appeal to your own words for testimony. Did you not yourself say that, at this time, the crown of Ammon is worn by your father, David?"

Solomon stopped short; she had a point. Technically, his father David had become the king of Ammon after defeating and annexing it, since no vassal ruler was installed. A moment later, the implication of it hit him also.

"My father is old; he is not taking wives," Solomon said. "Besides that, you can not be both the queen of Milchom and the queen of Israel."

"Why not?" she asked, leaning forward.

Solomon shook his head. "You would not understand. It is not done in Israel."

"Sovereignty again, I suppose?"

"No, not exactly, and the explanation may take longer than your patience can bear. But in Israel, there are no 'marriages to the gods.'"

"Well, then, perhaps a king could be restored to Ammon?" she suggested, her reasonable answer tinted with a hint of desperation.

Solomon pondered the suggestion for a moment while Naamah waited. He was finding himself truly interested in the conversation. He was discerning within her a well-concealed desperation. This was not merely recreational banter for the young princess, for a dark and terrifying cloud hung over her future, forcing upon her mind a singular kind of focus that only someone in her position could understand. When he did not respond, she put words to the question that was rising in her mind.

"Do you not agree that we who have made our home in this

land for centuries deserve our own State?"

Solomon shook his head again. "You do not understand. It is not in the power of Israelite kings to bestow land as though it were their rightful possession. The land belongs to Jehovah; we are simply the caretakers of it."

"But it certainly seemed in your father's power to *take* the land."

"You misunderstand," Solomon said. "My father could take no land that the Lord had not already appointed to him, and this had already been ordained centuries ago."

Naamah's silence was deep. When she finally did respond her tone was resolute.

"You insult me. You claim I do not understand. But I understand better than you know, for in your own scriptures the story is told. I understand who the land belonged to from the first, and now you occupy it by force. And now you presume to vilify our religion, when it was your own nation that set up the tradition of human sacrifice that we now follow? Do not deny it!"

Solomon blinked, aghast.

"A thousand undeserved pardons, my dear friend, but your meaning escapes me! *What* human sacrifice?"

"Do not toy with me. We know your history, though you think us ignorant. The story is told often, how Jephthah invaded and overcame us, though we were living peacefully as a neighbor to Israel in what for centuries was our rightful territory. After Jephthah brutally butchered our fathers, he sacrificed his own daughter to your god. So it has been with selected virgin daughters of Ammon ever since. You are to thank for my fate, Israelite."

Her voice was even, but a reddish tinge in her cheeks revealed barely-controlled anger.

Solomon could not believe what he was hearing. He knew that other nations had a less-than-perfect understanding of the God of Israel, but he had no idea the misinformation extended

26

this far. He regarded the woman before him with a new compassion. She continued to remain there motionless, her deep breathing the only evidence of her boiling emotions. She would add nothing more.

Solomon sighed and rubbed his neck, his eyes wandering into the distance. There were so many errors in her accusation, all deeply wrapped in hot emotion. Deeply felt errors were the most difficult kind to correct. The situation demanded a most wise and careful response.

"Naamah, Naamah," Solomon said finally in a tone that returned none of the anger of her accusation while turning to look at her with compassion. His voice projected such paternal resonance that the woman looked up at him in surprise that it could emanate from such a young face.

"Naamah," he said one more time, "kindly allow me to show you something. Tell me, do you like my garment?"

"Your . . . garment?"

He held out his arms for her to see.

"My garment. It is of the finest materials, exquisitely woven of one piece, custom-made for me. Is it not fine?"

"Yes, but why do you ask me this?"

"Look at this," he said, pulling back a fold to reveal a nasty rip where the fabric was soiled. She frowned and peered at the spot.

"How shameful. How did this happen?"

"I took a fall. And now what is otherwise a fine garment is spoiled by this damage. But it is just a garment—I have others. But you, Naamah, are like this garment. There are things that a person of your intelligence deserves to understand, but you have been badly served by a version of history that is not accurate. The lie rests unbecoming upon someone so keen of mind, as this tear is unbecoming upon a fine garment such as this. Yet, the situation need not remain so. I would very much like, if you would be so kind as to allow me, to present to you my version. There is nothing in the worship of the God of Israel that would ever subject you to the cruelty of human sacrifice."

The words of Solomon descended with such kindness that the very atmosphere around them seemed to change. Naamah felt it instantly—a sudden transformation, surreal and almost magical, covering her like a warm blanket—and was struck with a compulsion to hear his explanation even if she was skeptical. She stared, awestruck, at the young prince, feeling his warm eyes penetrate almost down to her soul. He had revealed a depth and compassion unexpected, fully incongruous with a person she had assumed was a privileged, pampered future king. While she hesitated, spellbound by the warmth of his entreaty, Solomon spoke again.

"Come, it draws cold out here. Let us go in. There is a warm drink prepared in Israel which friends share. If you will allow me the honor, I will prepare one for you, and we can speak about these things."

Naamah was sure she had never been spoken to so kindly in her entire life and could find nothing in her considerable arsenal of rhetorical skills to counter such abject courtesy. He had neutralized, in an instant, all the passion of the debate, extinguishing it in the honey of pure kindness. She was mesmerized. Feeling a lump forming in her throat, she nodded yes, not trusting her voice. Solomon's perception detected her emotion, but his kindness left it unnoted.

Chapter 4

Solomon seated Naamah near the fire. He proceeded to the server room of the guesthouse to prepare the promised drink, but also to fashion an argument fitted to the needs of the intelligent, but misinformed and desperate, Ammonite princess.

Naamah looked curiously after him, not understanding the emotions he had so quickly excited in her, nor the magic by which he projected such a disarming aura, but disliking none of it. What strange enchantments did this surprising young king wield, and what argument could he bring that could possibly answer her case—and her need?

Solomon returned shortly with two mugs, as well as an inkhorn and stylus, and a papyrus roll for writing. He sat down across from her, smiled warmly, and spoke.

"I have a story to tell you, Naamah, a story that I believe will bring much deserved relief to your mind, but my story may include points to which your excellent education will object. Therefore, I request that you agree to some conditions before I begin. If you wish to hear my story, you may ask no question, raise no objection whatsoever, until this mug is empty."

He placed a steaming mug before her. She could see that it was boiling hot and could not be touched for some time. She calculated how long she might need to sit and listen to the Israelite, and decided she trusted him enough to endure that long.

"Very well," she agreed, with a pursed smile. "Proceed."

Solomon quickly placed the papyrus on the table and sketched out a rough map of the area, speaking as he did so. "Here is Egypt . . . up here, Israel, Philistia, Phoenicia, Edom, Moab, and over here . . ."

"Ammon," she finished.

"No," Solomon replied. "Ammon . . . is over here." He drew a rough oval further up the map and to the west.

She frowned, began to open her mouth, then closed it again, remembering the rules of the conversation.

"Have you ever been to this area?" he asked, indicating the circle.

"Yes. My family has visited there often."

"What language do they speak?"

Her brow knit thoughtfully as she searched for his meaning.

"An Ammonite dialect. Why?"

"You have traveled there often, you said. Why?"

"My family has relatives in that area."

"Hmmm," Solomon replied. "You have relations in this area up here . . . right over here?" He pointed to the map again, tapping the spot with the stylus. "How and when did they get there?"

She stared at his map, shaking her head.

"You see, Naamah, the land of Ammon was originally farther north. That is why you still have relations there. The land where you live now was Amo-*rite* land, going far back into antiquity. The Amorites were conquered, and when they were, some of your people relocated to where you now live. Do you know who conquered the Amorites?"

She shook her head again.

"Do you know *why* they were conquered?"

It was an unusual question. The obvious answer was that the army of the invader was greater than the army of the defender, but she was quite sure that this was not the answer he was looking for. She offered no answer. He continued.

"When my fathers came up from Egypt, there were several lands that we were commanded by our God not to conquer," he said, tapping the map in three places. "Edom, Moab, and Ammon—but even so, the Ammonites did not allow our fathers to even pass through their land peacefully. We had to travel through the wilderness around them. In addition, your Ammonite forefathers conspired to make us disobey the commandments of our God, through the guile of the prophet Balaam. For this, a curse was put upon the people of Ammon. This curse was not unto death, but did prevent the Ammonites from joining the Israelites in worship. The Ammonites were banned from approaching Jehovah in the congregation of Israel for ten generations, of which about five or six have passed by this time. It may be that in our lifetimes, the first children will be born beyond that curse. But the curse itself is testimony that your people were originally *intended* to worship with the Israelites, if they so wished. Therefore, Jehovah, not Milchom, was the original God of Ammon."

Naamah's dark eyes shifted in thought.

"But the Amorites—" Solomon continued, "they were given no such opportunity. Like the Amalekites, they were to be driven out completely, which is exactly what happened to Sihon, their king, who at that time reigned in the original land of Ammon. And the reason they were to be driven out was punishment— punishment for all their abominations, the most heinous of which . . . was human sacrifice."

Naamah looked up sharply. Solomon nodded knowingly.

"This punishment God had foretold many generations before to our father Abraham. Not only did our God not command human sacrifice, He destroyed the nations that practiced it, using Israel as His instrument—but not before allowing them four-hundred years, from Abraham to Moses, to repent, which kindness they despised."

31

She studied his eyes, her interest growing more sincere by the moment.

"Now," he continued, speaking more briskly, "this land where you dwell is once again conquered, this time by Israel, and not only it, but the original Ammonite land farther west. Why? Because your people, once again, are practicing the abominations that caused the land to be conquered in the first place. Be assured, our people have nothing against the Ammonites. As I said before, we were commanded not to harm them; they are our relatives, as Lot was a nephew to Abraham.

You say the Ammonites deserve a State of their own. I say that the God of Israel agrees with you, and He even promises you a State of your own, provided you meet his conditions. According to our Law, Jehovah gave to Ammon all of this land, all the way up to the river Jabbok. Your nation can enjoy an inheritance just as Israel, but only if these cruel acts of heathen worship cease. Did your teachers ever tell you that Jehovah promises an allotment of land to your people, just as He promised an allotment to Israel? And if His promises have been realized by Israel, they can be realized by Ammon, for their source is the same."

Solomon paused, letting the point sink in. Naamah remained quiet, in the still tenseness of deep thought. Solomon continued.

"So, how did your people come to be scattered as they are? After our fathers drove out the Amorites, they did not settle in the land, but moved on to fight other battles. So some of your fathers moved in and annexed it as their own, living in houses they did not build, and reaping vineyards they did not plant. But the land was not theirs to begin with. Your fathers were given another mission. The land that ought to be yours now—this land I have drawn here—was the land of the Zamzummim originally, the giants, which God commanded your fathers to drive out, just as he commanded us to drive out the Amorites. But instead, your fathers scattered about and intermarried with the Amorites, and even served their king, Sihon."

Suddenly, he reached out and grabbed her by the wrist, surprising her.

"Look at your skin. You are much darker than I, even though we are both relations to Abraham. Why? Your ancestors intermarried with the Amorites! It was the Amorites who taught your fathers the ways of Milchom, his cruel practice of human sacrifice that threatens your life now! The God of Israel is not your enemy—He is your friend! It was His desire to protect innocent daughters like you that was behind our conquest of the land. But when King Sihon was driven out and our people did not immediately settle there, some of your fathers moved in. *That* is how you got there."

Her mind was reeling.

"But now this land is a vassal to Israel," he continued. "Why? Indeed, your people may have been allowed to remain a sovereign nation if they had not taken up the abominations of Milchom. And even today, if your people will renounce these evil ways, they may yet receive a sovereign kingdom back—up in the north, in your original land, the land which the God of Israel gave to you." Solomon referred again to the map he had drawn.

Naamah could no longer hold her silence.

"Wait . . . Am I to understand that it is because the Ammonites sacrifice virgin daughters to Milchom that your God has made our land a vassal to Israel? And if this practice is abandoned, Ammon will be sovereign again?"

Solomon nodded slowly.

"That is the promise of the God of Israel to you. This is a spiritual principle, and it does not apply to you only, but also to us. In the same way, if our people forget the God of Israel and begin to practice as you do, our sovereignty will be removed just as surely. For as I told you, the land is neither yours nor ours; it is the possession of the God who created it, and He grants it to them who please Him. This is why the history of our two nations is so inconsistent concerning this land. Time and again we have possessed it, and time and again your people have. Sometimes we are sent by God to punish you, sometimes you to punish us, for as I have said, the land is neither yours nor ours, but God's. Research the history; you will find that in each and every battle, the nation that won was the nation that was obeying the commandments of our God. Would this be a coincidence?" he asked, still firmly holding her wrist.

Naamah stared into his eyes spellbound. Though his version was completely different from the history she had been taught, she recognized instantly the internal logic of it and the fact that it explained so many things, including the existence of an Ammonite-speaking community in the northern region—and her dark skin.

Solomon released her hand finally, and leaned back to deliver the conclusion.

"Now, as far as Jephthah[3] is concerned, it is true that his daughter was killed—*not sacrificed*, but killed—and that, for a foolish vow. He had vowed before God that if he was victorious in battle, whatever came to meet him when he returned he would offer to God. To his horror, it was his daughter, his only daughter, who came forth that fateful day, with timbrels and dancing. It was a terrible thing, terrible—a blight on the record of a great man in our history. You see, vows made to the God of Israel can never be broken, no matter how foolish. That is why a person ought never to utter anything hastily before God. The lesson is this: God is in heaven and you are on earth—let your words be few! When you make a vow to God, do not delay to pay it, for He has no pleasure in fools. Pay what you have vowed—or better not to vow than to vow and not pay!"

Somewhere in the course of Solomon's detailed discourse, Naamah forgot that she was speaking to a boy several years her junior and found herself caught up as though it were a wise sage who was instructing her. She nodded slowly, trying to absorb all the new information. Solomon glanced over at her cup, from which no steam at all was emanating. She had not yet touched it.

"It appears I still have my full time left," Solomon quipped.

She looked over at her mug and was forced to smile.

"I am going to have to think about all of this," she said finally, shaking her head in wonder.

"I would expect no less than that a person of your intelligence would verify my claims before believing them," he replied. "And when you come to Israel, I can assist you in that effort. I can display to you the legal records from which this history comes. We can open the histories and read—in fact, I will show you in our own ancient scriptures where our God promised your people their own land. Would that be interesting to you?"

"No one has ever told me these things before. I would be fascinated to see if you could actually show me such a thing, but…"

"But what?"

"But I am afraid I am not coming to Israel."

"What? Why not?"

"I happened to be here in Egypt with my family on other business. I was left here for the convenience of my father, who did not want to have to tend to me. But in a short while, I will be going back to Ammon, or. . . wherever it is I live," she added.

"Israel," Solomon answered. "The land in which you live is in the territory that God gave to our fathers."

"Well, if that is so, then I *am* going to Israel after all, which means that I may see you again," she said.

"Yes," Solomon said, his eyes brightening, "I suppose it is possible."

Solomon and Naamah continued to talk late into the evening, about politics, history, religion—many things that Solomon loved to discuss but rarely found a partner both willing and worthy to speak with on his level. She, in turn, was duly impressed with the young king-to-be, who was able to provide sensible answers to many things that had been troubling her. Having quickly made headway on the difficult subject of the feud between their two nations, they found themselves getting along quite splendidly.

For the remainder of their time in Egypt, Naamah and Solomon remained in close proximity to each other. Solomon found each conversation with her as interesting as the first. She proved that the depth he had perceived in her in their first encounter was genuine. Her attention afforded him a measure of relief from the embarrassing behavior of Chavah—something for which he was grateful. Without Naamah, the trip for him might have been thoroughly miserable.

He became accustomed to Naamah's graceful, cat-like presence. Dark, often motionless, intelligent, and never far away, she was comforting even in silence—like a living, breathing piece of artwork which blended naturally into the environment around it, adding a calming effect by its simple presence. She was *everything* that Chavah was not.

It occurred to Solomon that Naamah would make a formidable ally in any situation. When it was time to leave Egypt, Solomon had truly found a friend in this unusual Ammonitess, though a respectful friendship was the full extent of their relationship. In a well-practiced habit of mind, Solomon dismissed quickly the inner whisper that asked him if the same could be said of Chavah and her Egyptian prince.

It was with a tinge of melancholy that Solomon left the guesthouse on the final day of the exchange, wondering if he would ever see Naamah again. He looked for her as preparations for departure were being made that morning, but she was nowhere to be seen.

As Solomon waited to board his ship, Naamah emerged from the crowd and glided stealthily up from behind, pressing close to get a message right into his ear above the noise of the crowd and the growing sea-wind.

"Please remember me when you come into your kingdom," she whispered. "I could be a much better wife to you than she, for though she is an Israelite, she is not your equal, but a mere child. But I understand your mind—you *know* that I do. Yet, if you choose to forget me, you know what my fate will be."

Solomon blinked, but did not turn. In a short time, he would be back in his own land where any friendship with an Ammonitess was highly unlikely to occur and, if it did occur, would most certainly not be received favorably. The past two weeks had had a dreamlike quality—a different place, different rules. He must not believe that he could import them to Israel. The trip was over. He knew that the needs of his coming office might force him to forget her. If that was what was required, that was what he would strive to do, but at the moment, he was not sure it would be possible. At Solomon's tender age, Naamah had, by her mature manner and womanly physique, come to represent his first blush of natural attraction to a woman.

Just as Naamah was beginning to pull away, Solomon turned his head and spoke.

"It is better to not vow than to vow and not pay."

She froze. It was not a "yes," but it was not a "no" either. Quickly, she left his presence, afraid to see him go, afraid of what emotions her face might reveal, and, above all, afraid of what her future held.

Solomon was afraid for her also.

Chapter 5

The wedding of Solomon and Naamah was inevitable, but the ceremony subdued. To take a foreign wife was politically dangerous for any Israelite king, and even more so for a young king early in his reign. Solomon tried to keep the matter quiet, but it could not be hidden completely, and uncomfortable whispers followed in the streets of Jerusalem, whispers which did not escape the notice of the king himself. But, having saved her life, and taken a wife he truly did esteem as worthy, Solomon returned to his duties, while Naamah was given a home outside the city.

Exactly one year following their wedding, Naamah entered the palace for only the second time since she had become Solomon's wife. Though she was grateful to him for saving her life, she was saddened by the politics that banished her to reside outside the city. She had learned a fair amount about the God of Israel in her first year, her quick mind absorbing the politics of the situation, even if the God of the land remained somewhat mysterious to her. She actually saw Solomon only once or twice a week, as often as he could make it out to her home, for he had instructed her that it was better for all if he went to her than for her to come into the Holy City.

The short visits that he could grant to her and their baby son were warm and happy. The connection they had made in Egypt turned out to be more than just youthful infatuation. Their minds did indeed work similarly. He would often compliment her by asking her opinion on various matters related to his office. She believed that he truly valued her thoughts, and she was correct. Of all of Solomon's advisers, Naamah was in a unique position: there was nothing for her to gain or lose by virtue of her counsel, her place being fixed. Considering what her fate would have been if she had remained in Ammon, she determined to be grateful, even if her marriage was less than a woman might desire.

Today, Naamah was about to test the strength of that marriage with the revelation of a secret she had deliberately withheld from Solomon, gambling that, at a later date, she would know better how to reveal it to him. Today, she had brought a guest with her, a guest that Solomon was not expecting.

Solomon spent the morning eagerly looking forward to the arrival of Naamah. His schedule was busy, and he could foresee by the current state of his affairs that he might not have time to visit her for several days. The chance to meet with her in the palace was a rare treat. He had arranged for a noon meal that they could share together in his private chamber. He dismissed himself from a morning meeting early, after giving those who remained instructions on how to conclude its business, and went to prepare for Naamah's arrival. Solomon was an accomplished chef and enjoyed cooking when he had the time for it. He had decided to prepare their meal himself, and share it with her in his private quarters.

Presently, there was a knock on the door, and a guard announced her presence.

"Come," Solomon said simply, inserting gruff unfamiliarity into his voice for the benefit of the guard.

He heard the door open and close and stood to meet Naamah, who would soon round the corner where a large indoor palm marked the transition between the entryway and the dwelling area proper. When she appeared, Solomon broke into a pleased smile and held out his hands toward her.

"Welcome, Naamah."

She glanced at him and took a step forward, then stopped, looking back toward the door. Solomon frowned, following her gaze. A moment later, another person stepped timidly into the room. Solomon saw it was a young woman, one he did not recognize. Naamah reached out and took the young woman's hand, pulling her fully into the room. Solomon looked from Naamah to the unexpected visitor with surprise. The girl looked back at him shyly, then cast her eyes to the floor. She was dressed in very fine, but unusual, apparel, a sleeveless white silk garment of unknown origin with golden embroidery throughout and a golden waist sash. She had been carefully decorated with jewelry, fine earrings, and many bracelets scattered up to her petite biceps. A modest but finely crafted tiara was upon her head. The brightness of her silk contrasted sharply with her dark Arabian arms. She was thin and well-proportioned, her hair was black and braided with many fine braids, and her face had been carefully painted to highlight her eyes and lips. Her skin, her appearance, her expression—everything about her revealed tender youth.

"My lord, the king," Naamah said, "may I present to you Adma, queen virgin of Milchom."

The girl dropped to her knees and bowed low with her face to the floor before Solomon. Solomon peered curiously at the pretty little visitor, then turned his eyes back to meet Naamah's, who treated him to one of her trademark deep, silent gazes. A few moments of silence followed Naamah's introduction, and Solomon observed that the girl was actually trembling on the cold polished floor. She was obviously terrified. Naamah motioned with her eyes toward the girl, as if to say Solomon should say something to her.

"Uh, it is my pleasure to meet you," Solomon said, giving Naamah a curious look. Then he stepped forward and, taking the girl's hand, lifted her to her feet. "Please, come sit with us."

The girl stood but still kept her eyes fixed on the floor. The three walked over to the couches where Solomon had arranged the food on a low table. Solomon reclined at his usual couch, and Naamah found a place across from him, the girl clinging to her side.

"Naamah, this is an acquaintance of yours from the land of Ammon, no doubt. To what do we owe the pleasure of her visit?" he asked.

Naamah took a deep breath.

"We owe her visit to the fact that it has now been a full year since the high priest of Milchom last took a bride. He takes one every year—either he or Milchom himself."

"High priest of Milchom?" Solomon asked. "What does he have to do with . . . ?"

Then the meaning hit him.

"Naamah!" he exclaimed, his eyes growing wide.

"To my father and all those in Ammon, even those who sent this girl here today, *you* are the high priest of Milchom, a fact to which I owe my life and, now, also this girl, Adma."

At the mention of her name, the girl once again timidly raised her eyes to look at Solomon, this time holding her gaze a moment longer with desperate, childlike uncertainty. Solomon looked back and forth in shock between Naamah and the little Ammonite princess.

"I know what you are thinking, my lord," Naamah explained. "Believe me, I do, for I have not dwelt in Israel for a year and learned nothing. But I tell you this: Queen Adma's presence here as your wife need be known by no one. She can live with me outside the city, ostensibly as my handmaid, but for her life to be spared, you must send word to those who sent her here that the priest has accepted, and is pleased with, his new bride."

Solomon groaned, dropped his head, and began to rub his eyes, grimacing in internal conflict. The presence of Naamah in Jerusalem had been difficult enough to explain, and now this. And it had not escaped his notice that Naamah had said that the priest of Milchom takes a bride *every year!*

A strange new voice punctuated the silence for the first time.

"I have been well trained how I might be pleasing to you . . ." the girl said, trembling, then added, ". . . my lord," imitating

Naamah's form of address. He looked up at the girl, who tried to smile and then, blushing, looked back down at the floor, still trembling slightly.

Solomon sighed. "Naamah, you should have told me. You have been aware of this for some time—even from the beginning! You are a most devious and crafty woman."

"Have you not often remarked that for this cause you love me?"

"And so you wait until this poor creature is here in my presence to bring me such terrible news!"

At those words, the girl let out a horrified choking gasp and began to sniff.

"No, no, not you, child," he quickly added. "You are fine; you . . . you are . . . you are perfect; you are exactly what the high priest of Milchom would want." He flashed an irritated glance at Naamah. "But I am *not* the high priest of Milchom! I am the king of Israel and the servant of Jehovah! How can I possibly take you . . . and her . . . and another and another every year from this time hence? Is that what this is to become?"

The girl frowned, genuinely confused now.

"It may not seem possible now," Naamah admitted, "but time can ease the situation in gradually. Ten years could easily pass before anyone knows there is a wife other than me. I could simply need handmaids. They can be kept outside the city, just as I am. But if this child takes back to Ammon the testimony that she just heard, that you are *not* the high priest of Milchom, she goes back to her death, and another innocent one like her will perish each year at this time until there is a high priest again. Does your own convenience justify the spilling of so much innocent blood?"

Solomon sighed, shook his head, and got up to wander over to the window, looking out through the lattice. The girl was about to speak again, but Naamah quickly hushed her, taking her by the hand. For a few minutes Solomon continued to brood by the window while Naamah and Adma waited in silence. Finally, he spoke.

"Certainly we can not send this poor creature back to her death."

Naamah and Adma exchanged excited glances.

"But we must find another way in the future," he added, still gazing outside.

"I will help you explore other ways," Naamah assured him. "My only request is that you bestow some relief to this woman now—assure her that her place here is secure—and we will leave that problem for another day. She has traveled far and, until now, has lived a life of desperation. Believe me, I know."

Solomon turned and looked back at the couch where the women were seated. Naamah, with her deep, quiet gaze, the picture of poised maturity, making the girl who sat next to her appear more like a daughter, though they were actually no more than a year apart. Naamah had been gracious in referring to her as a "woman." Nonetheless, Solomon observed that the girl was attractive—and more so, now that she had calmed down a bit.

"Very well," he said with resignation. "Adma, I welcome you to the land of Israel. You are accepted as my . . . my queen."

The words sounded strange to his own ears, spoken to someone he had only met a few minutes prior. He lifted an instructive finger.

"Naamah will teach you what you must know to survive here. I encourage you to pay attention to her, for the situation is not as simple as you may have been expecting."

Adma looked up at him while Solomon nervously shifted his feet, not knowing quite what else to say. Naamah caught his eye and sent him a silent message. Solomon stepped forward and took the girl by the hand, raising her to her feet before him.

"You are a most welcome and pleasing addition to my family," he said kindly, bending down to kiss her on the cheek as he cast a glance at Naamah. Naamah nodded with approval.

The girl blushed and flashed a full smile back up at him, revealing even more natural beauty than he had yet noticed.

"Thank you, my lord," she said more confidently. "I will not disappoint you."

"I am certain you won't," Solomon replied, adding under his breath, "*For that, you would have to see me.*"

Solomon was not optimistic about Naamah's ability to find an acceptable alternative in the future. For all of her intelligence, she had difficulty understanding the demands of the Israelite religion. He wondered if she would ever fully absorb it. Naamah was an agreeable companion, a good and interesting conversationalist, a wise counselor—in many ways a good fit for him. But there was a part of him—a most important part—where he and she had no commerce at all. The core of Solomon's being revolved around his God, a God who was a mystery to Naamah, all of her intelligence notwithstanding. Solomon felt acutely in his own heart the vacuum left by the absence of spiritual fellowship with his Ammonite wife.

****

The vision ended abruptly, replaced by the blur of landscape, as Solomon found himself back in the present . . . falling . . . rushing toward impact. Suddenly he glimpsed the form of a large boulder, its rugged topside hurtling toward him! He twisted his body to avoid it, and branches of plants grasped at him from several directions, throwing him into rotation. A thousand snapping twigs later, he crunched to a sudden halt at the bottom, the impact releasing all the air from his lungs, the rush of wind in his ears replaced by sudden silence. He found himself looking up through twisted vines at a starlit sky as several leaves floated down toward him.

I am alive.

The brush had broken his fall enough to render it unfatal. His surroundings came into focus. In his peripheral vision he perceived the ridge from which he had fallen, and his mind whirled in instinctive calculation. *I can not have fallen for more than four seconds; I can not be badly hurt.* A thousand thoughts followed on its heels. *What tripped me? Where are my guards? Can I walk? What an unlikely place to find myself—a king—at the bottom of a ravine, alone in the*

The powerful visions he had just experienced lingered, like strong dreams after a quick awakening. Gradually, reality pushed the visions aside, and the series of events that had resulted in his tangled recline in the hyssop bush came to remembrance.

He had been traveling. He was on a journey to Tyre, a city to the north of Israel, accompanied by just two guards. For the safety of the secretly traveling king, the wilderness trail rather than the valley road had been chosen to avoid encounters. The party had pushed ahead unrelenting that day until the light began to fade, and then had chosen a place on the mountain called Little Hermon to set up camp for the night.

After all was arranged, Solomon had left his tent, prodded into needless movement by the restless demands of depression. It was this walk that had ended in his present predicament. After hiking a distance of several bowshots from camp, he had found himself at the rounded crown of the Hill of Moreh, staring blankly over the Jezreel Valley as evening chased the sun over the horizon.

His two guards, Jachin and Boaz, were not far away; they had left camp temporarily to scout out the best watch points for the night, and Solomon had wandered. From his vantage point on the hill, he could see the fertile valley spreading before him. Far out in its haze, he saw a glow that he took to be the city of Jezreel, and just below him, the torchlights of the little backwater town of Shunem twinkled in an irregular circle. To his right, the sun was sinking slowly, blurring into the haze like a melting orange. A cool wind rushed up from the valley, drenched with the sweet smells of harvest crops.

The scene, though ruggedly beautiful, had provided no balm for his troubled soul as he gazed, his mind elsewhere. While he was so engaged, he suddenly noticed something odd: a thin whitish line, visible on the hills and draws to his right, as though painted across them. What was it? His first thought was that it was a road or trail, cut into the hillsides, but there was something different about it. Puzzled, he squinted out, trying to identify the strange object in the fading light. He soon noticed that it—

46

whatever it was—was visible on both sides of him, showing up as a horizontal line on the hills to his left as well as to his right. A prick of curiosity overrode his inner torment. After musing upon the unknown phenomenon for several moments, he perceived that if he were to hike a short distance down the slope from where he was standing, he would likely intersect it. Drawn by intrigue, he worked his way downward.

A short time later, he found himself standing before a strange structure: a low rock wall composed of roughly cut stones, no more than a cubit in height, but many bowshots in length. He traced it with his eyes, left and right, seeing it descend into draws and reappear beyond, its white outline visible even in the quickly fading light. It disappeared from view in both directions beyond the farthest visible hillsides, without termination. This puzzling structure was certainly manmade. Too short for a fence, much too short for a wall, it appeared absolutely purposeless. He was just about to step over it to examine it from the other side when suddenly he was startled by the near cry of an eagle overhead. Looking quickly up, he stepped into a hole, twisting his ankle. Yelping in pain and hopping onto one foot, he had tripped over the low stone structure, and thus, he began his fall down the rocky slope. It was while in this fall that the visions had come: three powerful visions passing before his eyes in a few brief seconds of freefall.

Now, lying on his back staring upward, Solomon groaned in as much annoyance as pain, though his ankle was fairly throbbing. The scaly branches of hyssop brush cut his view of the sky into a jigsaw puzzle through which the three bright stars of the Orion belt twinkled.

I must be facing north.

A sharp stick was poking him in the back. He twisted away from it. His water flask broke, and he felt the sharp cut of cold liquid on his skin. He groaned again. It would take considerable effort to rise, untangle himself from his position in the bush, and get out to where he could walk. He suddenly felt tired. He did not think he was badly hurt, but it was now nearly dark, and his throbbing ankle would make travel on the uneven terrain painful in the light of day, let alone at night.

Would that I might just stay here and die.

The words had barely crossed his mind when wisdom scolded him for self-pity.

Wisdom, oh cruel mistress thou, remove from me thy needless torments!

The emotions that accompanied his recent visions lingered and propelled his mind to thoughts of Chavah. The very thought of her fanned his inner ache, instantly restoring it to full force.

This torment will follow me to the grave!

He rolled to his side and curled up, pulling his clothing tight around him against the night-chilled air. He sighed with a shudder. He could barely manage a few tears and a soft whimper, the more overt expressions of grief long spent, while his stomach turned in painful pangs.

My guards are close by. They will find me here in the morning—or a pile of bones next spring.

Thoughts of Chavah chased him, even as his tired mind drifted toward sleep. Chavah was the whole reason for his journey . . . the unspoken reason, though this was certainly guessed by some. She was also the reason for his depression, his wandering, and, now, his fall and his present position. Chavah was a part of Solomon; she could in no wise be forgotten. She invaded his emotions, his thoughts, even his dreams.

Chavah . . .

Chapter 6

A virtuous woman is a crown to her husband: but she that maketh ashamed is as rottenness in his bones.

—Proverbs 12:4

Chavah stood before the polished metal plate which bore her image, arranging her hair and fussing with her garment for the tenth time. Just around the corner, her handmaid was fiddling with something.

"Durah, I do wish you would hurry," Chavah said, glancing nervously at the door. "It may be fashionable to be late in some places, but Solomon does not value it. He insists on punctuality when meeting with foreign guests. If I do not appear at the door when he calls, he is cross with me."

"I am sorry, your highness. I did not realize I would be doing your hair three times tonight," Durah replied.

On the bench before Chavah was strewn an array of barrettes, combs and brushes, beauty potions, perfumes, ribbons, pins, floral decorations, accents, and numerous other unidentifiable objects meant to enhance beauty. Chavah had built up a sizable collection, trying to satisfy her desire for something new while staying within the limits of what would be acceptable to Solomon. She found those limits confining at times, and was occasionally frustrated at his lack of sense concerning the special needs of a queen. The foreign wives who attended these kinds of feasts often outshone her in their apparel and personal décor, a fact which she found unbecoming to the great kingdom Solomon was trying to create.

Israelite women had extra challenges. Chavah knew that the restrictions of her religion, as strictly interpreted by some, made it difficult to make a good showing among the noble ladies of other nations. Since highlighting the face with colors was considered strictly heathen, Israelite women had to rely on the more basic arts of wardrobe, jewelry, and hairstyling to keep pace. Chavah found this to be a decided disadvantage.

Durah's voice sounded from the adjacent room.

"You could wear the tiara. It would be easier to finish your hair if I did not have to do all of it."

Chavah looked over at the tiara. That had been another of her apparent mistakes. She had purchased it in hope from a Babylonian merchant, but then was disappointed to learn that Solomon was not pleased with it. He'd claimed, of all things, that the outfit was that of a Babylonian temple prostitute. Still, to her, the tiara was a splendid piece. She could understand not wearing the garment with which it belonged, but the tiara seemed most harmless by itself.

"It may come to that if you do not hurry," Chavah replied.

Chavah was looking over her gown. The tiara would, in fact, match her colors and give a little spice to what she thought was an otherwise drab base hue. She reached over and placed it on her head, turning before the reflection to get a view from different angles. She remembered why she had liked it. It added that one final touch that lifted an ordinary outfit into the extraordinary.

She sighed, pursing her lips. Solomon had not actually objected to the tiara in particular; he had reacted to the entire outfit. Without the whole of it, would he even recognize the tiara as having been part of it?

There was a knock on the door.

"Chavah?"

It was Solomon.

"I am almost ready," she called, quickly lowering the tiara.

"No hurry, my love. I am going to the portico to greet the guests. You may come down when you are ready."

She breathed a sigh of relief.

"Thank you—I will be down soon."

Chavah turned back to her mirror and, with lips pursed, glanced up and down at her reflection.

"Durah, do you remember that white silk gown with the gold accents?"

Silence. Durah's hands temporarily stopped whatever they were fiddling with.

"Oh, do not be angry with me, Durah. I just want to try it on, just for fun. We have a little extra time now."

"It's in the wardrobe behind you."

Chavah stood up and sliced her hands through the hanging garments. There were so many.

"Where?"

"It's on the left, about halfway down."

Chavah located the gown in question and pulled it out, looking it over while holding the tiara in her other hand. When the tiara passed over the gown, she caught her breath. Quite coincidentally, the headpiece's design and colors were striking against the white gown, complementing it even better than the one she was presently wearing.

"Just get ready to do some small braids, Durah," she said. "I think this is going to work."

Durah let out a sigh of relief. "You are wearing the tiara?"

"You have to see this!" Chavah exclaimed. "Come here a

51

moment."

Durah came around the corner to see Chavah holding the tiara in front of the gown. Her eyes widened and she put her hand over her mouth.

"I never would have thought! The tiara looks magnificent with that! How did you think of it?"

"It's a gift," Chavah replied, thinking, *If only I were free to use it more.*

"I'll get the pins for the braids. The gold ones would be nice, don't you think?" Durah asked.

"Gold and black," Chavah said.

"Right," she agreed, shaking her finger at Chavah with an expression that communicated full approval.

Working with Chavah was sometimes difficult, but Durah had to agree that the queen-to-be did have a talent. It was part of her artistic nature. She was also skilled in drawing portraits, as a singer, and as a sculptor. Given free rein to do what she wanted, she could shine ever so brightly.

Chavah slipped on the garment and placed the tiara on her head, posing for the reflection. She was not an un-beautiful woman. She still had just a touch of the charming little child in her face, but the rest of her features had matured into elegance, and, when properly attired, she would pass for a respectable queen in any land. Her personality added much to her appearance. If new acquaintances found Chavah plain on first sight, they simply had to see her smile once. Her eyes could absolutely dance. She could light up a room. Her locally famous laugh, not loud, but somehow sharp enough to be heard amid a crowd, cut tensions and changed the atmosphere around her. Her engaging personality outshone her appearance, and wherever she went, laughter was soon to follow, even if she did tend to push the limits of proper queenly decorum.

Meanwhile, Solomon stood in his private chamber facing the open window, stroking his beard, oblivious to the view before him. He had been carefully measuring the potential import of the feast he was about to host. In the royal court, every event, even a social one, had political undercurrents. Every act performed by the royal court was symbolic. Every passing statement made or not made, every expression sent or withheld, was presumed to carry layers of meaning as various as the individuals who tried to interpret them. Though the present feast had no open political billing, Solomon did very much want to finalize some hard-earned trust and goodwill among some of the attendees, but without compromising any of Israel's interests. It was a delicate balancing act.

Solomon had been studying history and had learned that in many of the historic attacks on Israel, the attacking army had mobilized and entered through the Valley of Esdraelon. He felt the need to install a permanent force there and at other points along the trading routes, but movements of that nature could be interpreted as preludes to aggression.

Solomon also understood that Israel was positioned at a crossroads of major trading routes, both a blessing and a potential danger. The political landscape had changed fundamentally when Israel took control of both the eastern and the western trading routes. The eastern corridor had been secured by David when he vassalized the nations east of the Jordan. The western, through Philistia, had been secured by Solomon himself. Now there remained no reasonable trading route from north to south outside of Israel. Solomon, realizing that this re-tipped all of the scales, now had to respond wisely to the benefits and challenges of the new arrangement.

Israel stood to gain profits from trading, if the traveling caravans continued to pass through as before. The problem was, caravans carried foreigners and, with them, influences from heathen lands—influences that Israel could not tolerate. Beyond that, a rumor had spread throughout the world that Solomon was drafting foreign residents in Israel into his labor force for construction of the Temple. Some foreign travelers considered this policy an insult to their countrymen, others even worse.

Solomon could not compromise the values of Israel, but he did want the message of his kingdom to spread, for he was committed to keeping the charge his father had given him: to model the worship of Jehovah to the nations. A strict closing of the borders was as undesirable as it was impractical, but implementing policies that would cause otherwise friendly merchants to hesitate to enter Israel could have just as negative an impact.

The truth was, foreign labor *was* being implemented for the construction of the Temple, according to a strategy that his father had conceived. It could not be constructed otherwise, without a crippling increase in taxes—something Solomon was unwilling to do. One of the most important purposes of the convention Solomon had been hosting for the past week was to open a dialog with the major mercantile players in the world to ease their unspoken tensions concerning Israel's policies. The feast of the present evening was the final event in a week of careful strategic diplomacy.

Wives and consorts were welcome for the final ceremony. In most eastern cultures, women dined separately from men, but in respect for the customs of some of his visitors, Solomon had made an exception. The presence of women at feasts such as this was a double-edged sword. On the one hand, it underscored the social nature of the event, maintaining a helpful "informal" atmosphere; on the other hand, their words and actions could, and often would, be taken as representative of the kingdom, even when they meant no such thing. Chavah, in particular, was a challenge for Solomon. He very much needed her at this feast, to represent the virtues of an Israelite wife, but he was praying and hoping that she would not do anything out of order, as she was wont to do.

Egyptian traders would be present, so Solomon had seen to it that Kemisi, the daughter of Pharaoh Siamon, who had been given to Solomon as wife, had been brought from her home outside the city to attend the feast. Also Naamah the Ammonitess, was present.

Both of these women were known at this time to be harboring tensions toward their husband-king since his policy of drafting foreigners into his labor force had become known. No doubt, complaints from their countrymen had reached their ears. Nonetheless, the absence of the foreign wives as international symbols of goodwill would be certainly noticed at a feast such as this. Bringing all of his wives to the banquet was impractical—indeed, many of them Solomon had never even met. He concluded that he could achieve his goal by bringing a small sampling. These wives, at least, were known quantities. Bathsheba was present, of course, and Solomon hoped the experienced royal mother would help keep the younger queens safely in check.

The silent presence of his assistant waiting in the open doorway behind him eventually penetrated Solomon's reverie. It was time to go. He passed the assistant, entered the hall, and immediately detected the rich smells drifting down from the dining area. The royal banquet hall had been carefully and knowledgeably decorated. Solomon had researched the cultures of his guests and had chosen furnishings designed to make them comfortable without including directly anything related to pagan worship. He suspected that travelers might be hungering for the diets of their homelands and so had selected dishes to satisfy those cravings. The result was a carefully crafted international smorgasbord of sights, smells, and tastes. Music and entertainment were also planned.

His bodyguards, Jachin and Boaz, had moved into position as soon as the king left his chambers. These two most trusted servants had conceded to downgrade their normal military attire to more casual apparel with the assurance that their weapons would still be available to them. Now they dutifully followed the king briskly down the hall toward the portico where he would meet his guests. Solomon's face revealed the confident concentration familiar to all his aides, his sharp, dark eyes focusing ahead as if penetrating the very doors at the far end of the hall down which he strode. His mind was already far ahead of his body.

His confidence, born of conclusions reached in mature deliberation, radiated from him, creating an atmosphere that inspired others to follow. It was no use trying to hurry those deliberations, as all who worked in the court well knew, but once he settled on a course and committed to action, he was unstoppable. There was nothing to do but follow or be left behind. He was a king who inspired followers more than he commanded them—a true leader.

Solomon had been notified that the first of the guests had passed the gates to the grounds and were proceeding toward the banquet hall. His intent was to meet each of his guests personally at the door and let servants usher them in; he himself would enter last, after all who were expected had arrived.

"Notify the reception team. I want the washers to be at their posts," he said. "I assume the escorts and ushers are ready?"

"They are waiting at the gate, my lord."

"And the food and wine?"

"The confectioners have assured us that all is ready."

"Good. Has Nathan arrived?"

The assistant hesitated.

"Not yet, my lord."

To this, Solomon responded with eloquent silence. Nathan the prophet, though always welcome and often invited, was the one person in the kingdom who could not necessarily be counted on to appear at the king's summons. It would remain to be seen if he would be present at this feast.

Suddenly, Solomon had to slow his pace as his mother Bathsheba appeared beside him. He could see a question in her eyes immediately.

"What is it, Mother?" he asked, uncomfortable to be slowing down.

"I have been told that Chavah is to perform. I know how important this ceremony is to you, and I would not want to repeat the debacle we had at the Spring festival . . ."

Solomon waved her off.

"I have already seen to that, Mother. I have been in contact with the director of music; I have approved every hymn that is to be sung. We will neither offend our guests nor embarrass our testimony with these songs. But . . ." He stopped suddenly, remembering something and taking her by the elbow to lean in close. "I have not yet seen what she plans to wear," he said, searching his mother's eyes.

"I have. I was just in her chamber moments ago. I did not have to correct her. It will be well."

"Good," he replied. "There are few greater motivations for non-cooperation than too much correction."

"Which is why I said nothing. She will not embarrass us this time."

Only those who knew Solomon very well could have read a nearly imperceptible expression of relief on his disciplined countenance.

"You are a blessing, Mother. And now, I need to be going," he said with a smile. He released his mother's elbow, gave her a quick kiss, and continued his march down the polished stone hallway with his human train in tow. Bathsheba looked after him with pride.

As Solomon and his entourage passed the large, arched opening to the grand hall, he glanced in and suddenly stopped in a lurch, causing the guards following him to nearly run into him. Inside the room, decorators were adding finishing touches, lighting lamps and candles. Several were on high ladders, working on the final placement of a large blue banner on which was a gold embroidery of the lion emblem of Judah. It hung over the platform where the musical performances would take place. Deftly, Solomon cut into the room.

"Too low!" he called out, loud enough to get the attention of everyone in the room. "The banner blocks the light from the wall lamps, casting a shadow over the dining area—" He broke off, his eye suddenly caught by the struggle of a diminutive servant girl overburdened with a large platter of candles. He took two large strides forward and balanced the platter with one hand, supporting part of its weight in the other.

"You there . . . Matiah," he called to a young man, "come

help this maiden."

The man stepped forward quickly. Turning back to the banner, Solomon commanded, "Get it just above the window arches!" Then, pausing to look around the hall, he raised a finger and called out a single word—"Atmosphere!"—and turned to stride out of the room.

Everyone within hearing range knew well the import the king placed behind that single word, for even without its mention, "atmosphere" seemed to follow this gifted king as if it were woven into his royal train.

Solomon had discerned in a glance the presence in the grand hall of all of his most important advisors. They had been briefed on the goals of the meeting and coached on how to approach and earn the trust of the merchants. He also noted the presence of ambassadors from the four vassal states that surrounded Israel: Ammon, Moab, Edom, and Midian. Solomon hoped and expected these would represent him well at this feast, for their tribes would benefit as much as Israel from increased trading. It was to these that he had first proposed the current effort, and upon his explaining the many benefits to them, they had enthusiastically cooperated . . . so far. But they were not without their doubts. Being paraded before the world was not always comfortable for a vassal, for though being aligned with Israel promised them a share in its prosperity, it also put their material means on display before a covetous world. Solomon responded by promising them protection from any kingdom that became uncomfortably ambitious.

Solomon and his entourage were now approaching the arched stone entry door. Beyond it spread the wide steps toward the outer gate. There the guests would enter after servants tended to their animals and helped with their parcels.

King Solomon and his aides proceeded down the steps. A long stone walkway lined with blossoming flowers and water pools behind stone benches, stretched between the palace and the gate. Near the gate a line of servants, dressed in fine, matching apparel, was waiting with basins and water for the washing of feet. Behind them was another row with towels and anointing oils.

Flowers were waiting for the noble ladies, and garlands for the men.

At the gate, Solomon began meeting his guests, greeting them in their own languages, exchanging gifts with them, welcoming them to his personal home, and engaging them in small talk about the goings-on in their respective countries. As usual, the foreign guests were impressed with the new Israelite king's wide range of general knowledge and understanding, but as he greeted each new party, he discerned that many were yet holding unspoken questions about his rigid and sometimes seemingly bigoted religious practices. Escorts conducted each guest party to the grand hall.

Prior to Solomon's arrival in the grand hall, Bathsheba, with a mother's insight keen to the mind of her son, was busy examining every detail, from the décor to the food to the dress of Solomon's wives. Suddenly, from across the room, she noted the change in Chavah's attire. Her eyes went wide with surprise. *That maiden!*

Bathsheba quickly excused herself from the group with which she was conversing and began making her way, with some difficulty, toward the queen-to-be, an endeavor made more challenging by the fact that her target kept moving, and by interruptions on several occasions by guests or servants offering comments or making requests. Finally, she was able to catch the eye of Benaiah, a trusted court advisor and warrior with a keen eye and strong spiritual sense, who had noticed her furtive movement in his direction. Bathsheba signaled to him with a pointed glance toward Chavah. She saw him look over, quickly leave his group, and move toward the queen-to-be. Bathsheba continued to snake her way through the crowd even as she saw Benaiah take Chavah by the elbow and speak in her ear.

Here goes. Please let it go without incident!

To Bathsheba's dismay, Chavah did not immediately move apart from the group with which she was cavorting, forcing Benaiah to speak to her less privately than he had surely intended. Bathsheba renewed her efforts to hasten to the scene and finally arrived, to Benaiah's obvious relief.

"Queen Chavah, I fear the servants have dishonored you!" Bathsheba called loudly into the group. "You have common flowers when a queen's garland was prepared for you!" she improvised, taking her by the elbow. "Come this way at once!"

Bathsheba continued directing Chavah forcefully, smiling at the group all the while. She knew that Chavah, once socially engaged, could only be pried away with difficulty, and only a strong intervention would have any chance of succeeding. Fortunately, she was able with her surprise approach to create a small space between Chavah and the guests and capitalized on it to hustle Chavah safely apart from them, even as the queen-to-be smiled and nodded over her shoulder at the man with whom she had last spoken. Once Bathsheba had Chavah aside, she went about the task of hastily setting the servants to work on a "queen's garland."

"One that includes a *headdress*!" she instructed a maidservant in a hushed but forceful voice. The maidservant blinked and then nodded, hastening toward a door.

Bathsheba looked nervously toward the door where Solomon would soon appear and, once again, caught the eye of Benaiah, who wiped mock perspiration from his forehead in response.

When Solomon finally arrived in the hall, he was happy to find the atmosphere of the preliminaries pleasantly social, the members of his administration rightly at work mixing with the merchants, but his keen eye quickly recorded the unsurprising absence of Nathan the prophet, as well as the curious absence of Chavah and Bathsheba. He took some time to mix among the conversing groups, sampling wine and encouraging guests to try grapes and other fruits from trays borne by tireless servants combing through the room. After some minutes, he noted the return of his mother and queen through a far doorway.

When the pace of the evening seemed to suggest it, the guests were invited to be seated, with Chavah, Naamah, and Kemisi positioned where they could converse with the foreign women. As the food was brought forth, Solomon himself called out the name of each dish, to the welcoming cheers and applause of guests from the region of the world from which the dish originated. He was carefully monitoring the pace of events. Later in the evening, some of the guests would be given the opportunity to speak, after which there would be music. He glanced over at his wives, attempting to read their faces.

Naamah was generally pleasant, engaging as usual in intelligent conversation, attracting as she often did the curious glances of nearby men who seemed surprised to hear such wit proceeding from the lips of a woman, not to mention a beautiful queen. But Solomon, in his quick glances in her direction from down the table, was not unaware of the sarcasm in her expressions and wondered if it was as apparent to others as to him.

Chavah and Kemisi, neither as intelligent nor as aware as Naamah, were oblivious to any such undertones and generally missed the underlying meanings in Naamah's comments. These two floated along the surface of most conversations, with the exception of Chavah's infatuation with the female fashions of foreign lands, a subject the depths of which she could continually explore without boredom. Solomon noticed her engaged in a lively conversation with two wives of a Neo-Hittite trader, her cheerful voice occasionally drifting like a chirping bird over the general noise of conversation. Now and again, men glanced over to find the source of the cheerful sound.

Solomon had noticed the unusual, and unfamiliar, garland that looped over Chavah's head and suspected it had something to do with the earlier absence of Chavah and Bathsheba. He made a note to investigate it at the next opportunity. In the meantime, the young king continued to impress, conversing freely with traders from every nation on issues both small and large. He had provided good wine but soon noticed an overly frequent refilling of chalices among some of the merchants and began to calculate a change in the order of events to prevent the feast from descending into delirium.

A trader named Temhunkut, a heavy-set—say it, *fat*—and very prosperous multi-national merchant of mixed origin, was becoming louder and more vocal in his comments as the wine loosened his tongue.

"In the days of King Saul and David," Solomon overheard him say, "we needed only to rely upon the tribes along the eastern route to protect us—in those days, we all remember, the protection was as much from Israel itself as it was from raiders. But today if Israel provides protection from the raiders, who then protects us from Israel?" His comments were loud enough to be heard by some nearby who temporarily dropped their conversations into lower tones.

"Let *us* deal with Israel," the ambassador from Ammon replied calmly. "Your protection is still secure with us, as ours is with Israel. Israel is not pursuing aggression, but peace."

Naamah the Ammonitess eyed the ambassador skeptically as he talked, while he avoided her glance, knowing she was thinking of the many Ammonites in Israel who had already been drafted into labor.

"I am certain that the Ammonite queen agrees with you," Temhunkut said sarcastically. "For who could not trust a king who would give his servants the untiring protection that can only be found under the eye of his whipmasters?"

Naamah glanced at Temhunkut, then looked away in disgust. Others in the room were beginning to catch the tone of the exchange.

"The current labor force is made up only of those foreigners who dwell within the tribal borders of Israel, west of the Jordan," said the Moabite ambassador who sat next to him. "They may leave Israel at any time and return to their own lands if they wish. There is no forced labor going on in any of our lands."

Temhunkut finished off his chalice and held it up to a servant who dutifully refilled it.

"Israel is what it wants to be among vassals," he declared. "For if the Israelite army is under control of the king, who is to say the king will not need *more* temples in *other* cities for the worship of his god, which will require more laborers? Such will not come from Israel, I am sure, and who do you suppose will carry his stones then?" He sloshed his chalice and threw back his head for another drink.

Then the steady voice of Solomon broke in.

"My friend, the God of Israel is One. As such, He is not in need of more than one Temple, any more than He needs more than one nation."

Though Solomon had replied calmly, at the voice of the king many heads turned from several seats down and across the table.

"Thusly it is written in our laws," he continued. "Israel has no ambitions of expansion. But if we are enjoying peace and prosperity in this hour, it is only because of our God's blessing. All who wish to be so blessed may also be—if they will honor His laws," he concluded with a smile.

The voice of Solomon had caught the attention of all in the hall who had not previously noticed the exchange, with the exception of Chavah who was still chattering away at the Hittite queens. Suddenly, as if on cue, a door opened at the far end of the hall and heads turned to see the empty space for a moment, followed by the appearance of a seemingly out-of-place old man dressed in rough wilderness attire and holding a staff. The room went silent. Nathan had arrived.

The keen eyes of Solomon quickly recognized the prophet. *He always arrives at precisely the right moment!*

The king quickly began to calculate all the new possible tangents now that the prophet had been added to the mix at this delicate moment, and did not notice Chavah slip up beside him to whisper in his ear at just the same instant.

"Dearest," he heard unexpectedly, "could you look for a moment at the two Hittite wives sitting over there? They have some colors on that I do so admire, and they tell me these dyes are available in their countries and we could have them here, too, if trading opens up. I just want to know if you would allow such things. I find them so attractive."

Solomon turned his head slightly sideways but kept his eyes on the far door, blinking in astonishment at being called upon to juggle such a delicate matter, while at the same time being asked by his queen to respond to such a trivial question. He glanced over at Chavah, who was peering back at him with sincere eyes, apparently unaware of anything else taking place.

"I'll speak to you about that in a moment, love," he whispered, then turned to face and greet Nathan the prophet.

Chavah frowned and then looked indignant before going back to her seat and fixing her eyes downward. She did not appear to notice Nathan's entrance.

"Distinguished guests," Solomon began, "it is my great pleasure to introduce to you one of Israel's wisest and most beloved citizens, the prophet, Nathan."

He raised his hand in greeting to the prophet. Nathan raised his hand in return and began shuffling toward the table, his confused escort following along behind, not knowing quite what to do. The guests peered curiously at the strangely dressed man, who apparently had made no effort to choose attire appropriate to the occasion.

"Nathan, an advisor to two Israelite kings now, is a frequent observer of the proceedings in this kingdom," Solomon explained. "His counsel is highly respected."

Nathan nodded to a few of the guests as he passed, his wise old eyes twinkling as he came to take a seat next to the king.

Temhunkut grunted irreverently.

"Counsel that would keep Jerusalem from becoming the international metropolis that the rhetoric of this gathering would suggest," he grumbled. The eyes of the room turned back toward the half-drunken trader.

Nathan's twinkling expression changed not a whit at the comment as he took his seat, looking back and forth at the dishes in the table's center as though he had not heard. Solomon chanced a quick glance at the prophet, then responded to Temhunkut.

"Israel has no qualm with any nation, my friend. We would be happy to entertain and assure safe passage to any trader who would come through our borders in peace; we only ask that our

God be respected, as you would want us to respect yours, were we in your land."

"One and only one god—that is the nub of the problem. For in any of our lands, your god would be welcome among all the rest of them, but in your land, it is he and he alone," Temhunkut said coldly.

Nathan was calmly dishing himself food, attempting to add nothing to the conversation, while Naamah, giving nothing away with her expressionless eyes, was understood by those who knew her to be hiding a torrent of thoughts. Chavah was only just beginning to get the gist of the exchange and was asking the ambassador seated next to her for further explanation. Kemisi looked back and forth nervously, not fully understanding the tension, but not liking it, while Bathsheba, more experienced in such events, leaned slightly forward, watching the drama for any opening where she might be able to assist.

Solomon replied to Temhunkut, "Only by this policy, friend, can Israel prosper. Other nations may be able to prosper, to a degree, with many gods, but Israel is not in such a position. Our God has chosen us, given us His covenant, and promised to bless us above what any other deity could, if we would honor Him. This places upon Israel a responsibility that other nations do not have. If it seems to you an undue burden, I would suggest that you consider our present prosperity. Has any other god done as much for his people? Our God is honoring His covenant with us, as are we with Him. It is for love of Him that we serve Him. That He requires our complete consecration is but a small price to pay for the many benefits of His blessings."

Temhunkut snorted.

"Consecration. Well, I will give you this: At least your consecration has allowed your wives more discretion than some past Israelite kings did. For, who among them would have allowed his queen to be presented in Babylonian attire?" And he raised his mug toward Chavah, then took a good long drink, finishing the remainder without a breath. The eyes of the room came upon Chavah.

Solomon paled, caught in a rare moment of surprise, perceiving that something must have occurred outside of his awareness. It somehow concerned Chavah, and perhaps was connected to that strange garland she wore. Chavah blushed, then smiled at the group, not knowing if she had been complimented or insulted. Bathsheba lowered her face into her hands.

All eyes turned back upon the king.

Something must be said...and now. Hesitation in this moment is as perilous as the wrong word!

"In Israel," Solomon said evenly, "we do not claim perfection in all of our goals, but simply require of ourselves that we continue to reach toward them. Nor do we demand perfection in any of our many friends, even you who are among us today. The grace we extend to ourselves, we also extend to you. So let us now go forth and prosper together!" he called loudly, expertly adjusting his tone to change the atmosphere.

The room let out a hearty cheer of agreement, happy to move past the tension of the moment. Temhunkut seemed to relax. Chavah smiled openly. Solomon was relieved. And Nathan sat expressionless.

"Bring forth the music!" Solomon called, clapping his hands twice, and a curtain was pulled back at the side of the room, where an ensemble that had been standing hurried to their seats and arranged their instruments. Chavah, surprised, arose from her chair.

There were supposed to have been acrobats and jugglers first, followed by an illusionist—whose every trick Solomon had already discerned in a private audition to ensure there was no real magic involved—and *then* Chavah was to sing. But Solomon's intention now was to simply move the agenda along. His sudden call for music put her on stage immediately, where she would solo on some carefully chosen Jewish hymns. Solomon felt a brief moment of panic. Had he acted too quickly? Could Chavah perform under the circumstances? There was something here not understood.

For the first time, Nathan the prophet moved with definite

purpose, signaling with his hand, and Solomon leaned over as the prophet whispered something in his ear. As the king listened, his expression changed almost imperceptibly, and he relaxed. Bathsheba noticed.

Chavah was taking to the stage. Solomon was aware of the redness on the back of her neck as she walked away from him toward the platform. Apparently the insult in Temhunkut's last comment had finally dawned upon her. Solomon had not meant to embarrass her, but it could hardly be avoided under the circumstances. She would have to perform, the awkwardness of the moment notwithstanding.

The music started. After a hesitant beginning, Chavah's natural gifts as a performer took over, and soon she was given over to the music, taking her audience on a tour of musical heights like an expert guide, as she had done so many times before. She had them all smiling and laughing before long, and the entire group agreed that the Israelite queen would be a desirable addition to any court. "Too bad she is an Israelite" was a comment frequently heard.

Following her performance, Chavah was warmly greeted by all, at times a bit more warmly than Solomon was comfortable with, but to her credit, she had changed the atmosphere of the event, a skill at which she was uniquely adept.

Solomon found himself thinking as he often did . . . *If only that gift could be channeled.*

Nathan slipped out as mysteriously as he had appeared, apparently having accomplished the one task for which he had come. Bathsheba excused herself early, pleading a headache. Naamah remained acceptably civil, and Kemisi seemed to enjoy a rare chance to spend some time away from her home of banishment outside the city. When the feast drew to a close, Solomon made the final speech, dismissing his guests with promises of a prosperous future friendship. The majority seemed receptive to his goodwill, welcome evidence that the evening's goals had been salvaged after a questionable beginning.

After escorting the last of his guests to the gate, Solomon

dismissed his guards and turned to slowly walk the stone path back to the palace alone. It was a clear spring night, and the sudden peace following an evening rich with noise felt delicious in his ears.

As he approached the steps, he heard muffled voices and turned to notice two figures seated on a bench to the side of the stairs under a grove of large ornamental palms. Bathsheba and Nathan the prophet evidently had not left the grounds after exiting the hall, but had remained here and were now engaged in a serious conversation. Solomon instinctively knew the subject under discussion. It was becoming harder to avoid every day. He changed his course to join them.

Nathan and Bathsheba could see Solomon's face as he drew near, illuminated by the torchlights bordering the palace stairs, but to him, their faces were dark. They fell noticeably silent upon his approach.

"It appears all that needs be said has been said," he offered to their silence.

Bathsheba glanced at Nathan, then back at Solomon. She had some inkling of her son's thoughts, but with the never-failing instinct of a mother, she had an even better read on his heart. He was quite torn up over the matter and did not need to be lectured.

"There were some important successes this evening, my son," she said. "Congratulations."

"Indeed," Solomon agreed and stepped forward to stand before them. "And some glaring failures, no doubt."

"Sit down a moment?"

Solomon sat on a rock wall that bordered a decorative pool opposite them and rubbed the back of his neck, relaxing for the first time in several hours.

"Have you spoken with Chavah yet?" Bathsheba asked.

"No."

"Perhaps you would like me to speak to her," his mother offered.

Solomon looked at her and hesitated. "If she will not hear me, how will she hear you? My whisper carries more weight in the kingdom than a shout to her. I am just too common to her, I'm afraid." He ran his long fingers through his dark wavy locks, staring at the ground. "But you are, of course, free to try," he added.

Nathan peered at the king, lowering his head. "Son, you well know that if talk could resolve this issue, it would have been resolved long ago. This is not a matter of the ears, but of the heart."

Solomon nodded. Nathan's words were true, but a lifetime of love and expectation was not easy to dismiss.

"I will speak to her again."

Nathan and Bathsheba exchanged a glance. The night breeze fluttered the torches behind them momentarily. Bathsheba cleared her throat. "Son, I understand that you very much want to do what is right for the kingdom, and also for Chavah. We all love her, of course."

"Of course," Solomon agreed, not sounding convinced.

Nathan seemed to send Bathsheba a silent message. She turned to Solomon, and asked an unexpected question. "Do you see my scarf here? The color of it, the style—have you seen one like this before?"

Solomon raised his gaze from the stones in front of him and looked at the lily-gold silken scarf his mother was holding out toward him.

"Your scarf? Of course, its like is seen throughout all Jerusalem. Nearly every maiden has one. Why?"

"They do now," she replied, "but they didn't used to. This, in fact, is the first one. I purchased it from a merchant in Tyre when your father and I traveled there once, years ago. I liked it, wore it often. It was not long before I began to see a similar style and color in the streets. I was queen. The daughters of Israel were watching me."

Solomon was nodding, knowing the direction her comment was going.

"Son, you have been king now for six years. The young men of Israel look to you as a model. But the daughters of Israel—they do not know whom to follow. You have taken no Israelite queen. What are they to do? Should they continue to follow me? Or Naamah? Or Kemisi, or one of . . . who knows how many others? If they do not have a clear example, they will take what is . . . before them, be it good or bad. The time is drawing near when you *must* take an Israelite queen."

"And we all know in whom that example is most absent, you mean to say," Solomon finished for her.

Nathan lifted an instructive finger.

"The queen of Israel represents the values of the kingdom, as does the king," Nathan explained, "as I am sure you know."

Solomon only nodded silently. He did know. He was just hoping that the Lord would visit Chavah, as He had visited him and had imparted to him a divine gift of wisdom. Honestly, before that encounter, Solomon knew he could not have had nearly the zeal for Jehovah that he did now. Chavah was not an evil woman; she had just had no such life-altering event. She was well taught, but she was lacking a personal experience with God. Solomon had been stalling and praying, but it was true—the situation could not be held in abeyance indefinitely. Already, evidence of Chavah's influence could be noticed among the daughters of Jerusalem, if one had discernment to see it, which Solomon did.

Solomon looked over at Nathan, taking a thoughtful pose. "Interesting, is it not?—to have been taught the Law from my youth, surrounded by it, immersed in it, like many lads in Israel, but still, never understanding it until its Author came and paid a personal visitation." He shook his head. "One moment in that presence will teach you more than a lifetime of learning from books. Chavah is the same as I, save this one indispensable difference." He looked directly at the prophet and paused thoughtfully.

The two were nodding at him.

"How much longer do I have?" he asked.

Nathan regarded the young king with his kind old eyes. He loved him, even as he had loved his father David, and discerned the turmoil in his heart.

"Jedidiah," he replied, "you are beloved of the Lord. So it has been spoken, and so it is. You have been divinely selected for your place as king. That ordination could not take place unless a fitting queen also existed in the mind of God, for the two make up a single thought. The queen that is needed to complete this kingdom will not be withheld from you. Only, you must surrender to God's perfect will in the matter and be willing to sacrifice whatever . . . must be sacrificed. I have no word from Jehovah for you. But I have every reason to expect that God's ordained queen will be presented to you in *this* season, before the completion of the Temple. And when you find her, there will remain no doubt in your heart."

Nathan's eyes projected the still confidence that was so familiar to those who knew him as he looked directly at—even *through*, it seemed—the young king.

"Perhaps I have her already," Solomon said.

"Perhaps," the prophet agreed. "But the fire must strike the altar—and it will."

"I take great comfort in that, and I am not unaware of these . . . issues—how could I be? In fact, as of this night, I have made a decision. I will no longer allow this matter to take its own course."

Nathan and Bathsheba looked at each other curiously, but Solomon offered no further explanation.

"If you will excuse me, I am tired. I appreciate your attendance at this important event, my father," he said to Nathan, "and your wise counsel concerning *all* the matters of the kingdom. I am in very great need of your continued prayers on the issues that stand before me. Mother," he said softly, stepping forward. Bathsheba leaned toward him and received a kiss on the cheek. "Know that I have heard you, and you serve me well, as always."

He turned to leave, slowly mounting the steps to the palace alone. Nathan and Bathsheba watched the elegant king as he left them, then their eyes connected. Bathsheba shrugged, partially in hope, but also in wonder about what the king had in mind to do. Nathan nodded to her, but revealed nothing, neither in his eyes nor with words.

In his private chamber, Solomon changed into more comfortable clothing but had no intention of retiring just yet. The incident with Chavah represented the boldest break with protocol he had yet seen from her. She was not getting better; she was getting worse. Her behavior could not simply be ignored, as he had been perceived as doing thus far.

He entered the palace yard again. His path this time took him off the stone walkway, through the grass, past the decorative pools, and into the orchard, after which he emerged in a clearing where the starry sky was visible. He took a few deep breaths, turned to look back, and then wandered back to sit on the edge of a pool.

What can I do with such a maiden?

He loved her—he had always loved her—but things were not the same now that he was king. He had responsibilities to the kingdom, to all of Israel, and to God. His eyes wandered over the scenery around him. He felt a pang of grief and wiped a few brief tears. She simply did not understand—that's all there was to it. And he could not make her understand. There was nothing to do but pray.

If I do not see changes in her soon, I will be required to . . . He hesitated to even think it. *I will have to replace her. I will have to find another queen.*

The wave of emotion swept back over him again. How could he do such a thing? What of the promise his father had made to her father, Chimham?

But then again, the promise was not that Chavah would be his *queen*, but his *wife*. He had always assumed she would be queen, but perhaps that had been presumption. After all these years, was Chavah destined to be simply wife and not queen? Though he knew it would technically meet the requirements of his father's vow, it would mean the painful death of his childhood dream— and hers.

He shook his head in inner resolve. He would not give her up without a fight; he would contend for her as long as possible. He was aware of the seriousness of the situation, even if she was not. It required extreme measures. Solomon had always advised against the making of vows, but under some circumstances it was not only justified, it was necessary. This seemed to be just such a case. The decision came upon him suddenly, as though dropped from above: He would take the Nazarite vow.

He knew the requirements. Under a Nazarite vow, a man would let his hair and beard grow untouched, not become defiled by contact with any dead body, and touch no fruit of the vine, be it wine, grapes, or even raisins, during the full term of the vow. At the end of the vow, his hair would be cut and presented to the Lord by the priest, the length of it signifying the time that had passed under the vow. The hair would be burned by the priest before the Lord, and various gifts and sacrifices would be offered. That was the process of the vow, but the particulars of the vow would be up to him. Solomon had never before been desperate enough to take such a vow, though he had seen others do so. He was keenly aware of the seriousness of it and the offense it would mean were he to slip from it. But he was facing, for the first time, a situation desperate enough to warrant it.

He wandered back out into the wooded area and knelt down before the Lord. A beautiful canopy of stars spread above him. He lifted his eyes to the heavens.

"Lord God of my fathers: Your servant's life is in your hands. This great kingdom, which is the heritage of Jacob, is but loaned to me. Only by honoring you may your unworthy servant keep it, but if your ways are despised, let it be given to another lest it become dishonored by my sins. Your wisdom, O God, has been my constant prayer, and your wisdom I now seek on this most important matter: It has been revealed to me that this kingdom must have a queen. The time is near when she must step forth. Yet, your servant knows not, after all these years, who she is to be. My vow now goes forth before you, O God: If Chavah is to be queen, arrest her heart, as you did mine. If another is to be queen, reveal her identity to your servant. Please hear me God, O God, and answer speedily. Your servant shall not cease from this vow until one of these two is accomplished."

Solomon remained there a long while, the sweet Judean Spring breeze playing with his hair and garments. The heavens remained painfully silent, while the wet grass soaked through his garments to cool his knees. Finally, he arose to return to the palace, slowly climbing back up the wide steps to meet the still silence of the sleeping palace. With emotions both hopeful and somber, he retired.

Chapter 7

The heart knoweth his own bitterness; and a stranger doth not intermeddle with his joy.

—Proverbs 14:10

Over the next few weeks, it became apparent to those in the court that Solomon had ceased trimming his beard. A short while later he was gently encouraged by his mother to get a haircut, which he declined without explanation. He went about his business as usual, effectively managing the kingdom and overseeing the building of the Temple, but those who knew him sensed a different spirit about him. He was somber, morose, often found staring into space, and avoiding participation in the normal feasts and fanfare in which he had been known to make merry. Something was wrong.

For all of Solomon's wisdom, his precise logic, and his incomparably ordered mind, the king was discovering that the deep well of emotion and passion that allowed him to write elegant songs and poetry also had a dark byproduct: He was capable of depression—and that of a depth not possible among men of ordinary mind. It was difficult—nay, impossible, it seemed—for him to shake himself of it. He spent more time in solitude so as not to trouble others with his own low spirits. He slipped away from the palace often to spend hours alone at the interesting new home he had been constructing on the far side of the grounds. There he could escape the constant questioning that pressed upon him.

Chavah had known that this house was being built for her. Though she was concerned with Solomon's brooding—even she could not shake him of it—she never doubted his love for her, even when he pulled away and seemed distant. She amused herself with her crafts, being led by her artistic gifts into bold new areas. She would travel among the street markets, examining various works from other nations and using them as inspirations for her own creations. On several occasions, she considered taking a tour of other cities to see what could be found there also, reasoning that this might allow Solomon some needed space right now.

Solomon had always had a serious side, but she had never seen him so somber before. For the first time in her life, try as she might, she could not impact him, distract him, make him smile and laugh. *He will come to himself,* she reminded herself, remembering that, eventually, he always had. Occasionally, she wondered if it were some failing of her own that had led to his silence, but dismissed the idea. If, perchance, she did have pause to doubt his feelings for her, she need only return to the new house he was building for her, where his love for her was etched into every wall.

Solomon had designed the house on the model of a vine, with rooms sprawling out gracefully from a central hallway. Its moldings were decorated with images of ripe grape clusters on leafy vines. It was elegant and beautiful. There were, however, some curious aspects to the house that were kept secret, even from Chavah. Solomon had explained that the entire house— every facet, every room—was designed for some particular purpose, each of which would be revealed to her as they lived their lives together.

One central chamber opened into a heptagon with seven high walls, and the roof was of colored glass. Solomon was knowledgeable in astronomy. The room was so situated that as the sun traveled across the sky, it would cascade the room in seven colorful hues in the order of the rainbow. Inset into each of the high walls were elaborate display cases and shelving made of the finest wood and metal, cedar and gold. Interesting they were, but empty. Each of the seven walls featured a design and color scheme unique to itself, yet blending with the others. As the day moved forth, it was as though the room were alive, changing from hour to hour as the color flooded through the skylights, highlighting one surface after another, and then blending into the next color to highlight the adjacent wall. This chamber itself had taken four years to design, requiring careful observation of the sun's movements through all the seasons. The actual construction had taken two years, and then it was observed for two full solar seasons to fine-tune the many mirrors which helped cast the light. This was, then, the fifth year since the idea's conception; Solomon had begun it when he was sixteen years old.

It was equally marvelous at night as the phases of the moon marched in a small circular pattern of light when observed at the same time each night. At the very peak of the chamber was a small area of clear glass—crystal, the most rare and expensive of stones—and sizeable enough pieces had been found, somewhere, to act as windows. Through these, the twelve constellations would pass, marking the months of the year. The four cardinal points of the year were also marked, two solstices and two equinoxes, as a single shaft of light passed through a carefully placed ring of diamonds and illuminated shiny medallions on the opposing wall. Gold for summer, copper for fall, silver for winter, and topaz for spring.

It was a wonder—a truly magnificent place!—and one could sit for hours and watch the drama of light unfold, breathtaking even while playing upon the curiously empty compartments. Chavah very much liked the place, though it was obviously unfinished. Solomon called it the "worship chamber." She sometimes wondered if she could add some contribution to it.

The worship aspect of the chamber had been settled in consultation with the prophet Nathan, who had blessed it at Solomon's request and confirmed that its inspiration had come from God. In it were to be housed specially crafted memorabilia commemorating the seven yearly feasts: Passover, Unleavened

Bread, Firstfruits, Weeks, Trumpets, Day of Atonement, and Tabernacles. The room was designed to record a life's devotion to God through these feasts, with each year's celebrations marked by the placing of a carefully designed token in its pre-determined location. Each piece had already been designed, and the room so configured to receive it that, once placed in its chamber, it would contribute a new harmony to the symphony of light. Pieces from the early years would be placed in the lower compartments, and as the married couple advanced in age, their memorabilia would circle up the chamber walls, blending at last into the glorious light in the pinnacle, which represented their entrance into the hand of God at life's end. Each item placed therein would summon a sacred memory, reinforcing loving devotion to God, like a tower of faithfulness—brick upon brick.

If this room represented the pinnacle of worship, the whole house followed suit. There were no accidents in design anywhere. Everything had a meaning and a purpose, but the purposes could only be fulfilled through the lives of the residents of the house, as husband and wife.

Now, as Solomon became gloomier, and the palace residents' concern for him grew, Chavah began to be impressed with a sense of desperation. If she had any gift at all, she knew, it was to dispel gloominess and bring joy to a situation—or to a person. She found this reinforced wherever she went, for no matter where she wandered, joy and laughter were soon to follow. And she believed that there was no person to whom she was more charged to bring joy than Solomon. She began to see, in his depression, a failure in her own duty. She could not understand him; she had resigned herself to that years ago. She could not meet his mind, as Naamah did. Nor could she ever match the stunning beauty of Kemisi. But one thing she could always do was to make him smile. She took pride in that. His apparent depression became a burden to her, and a challenge. She determined not to let this thing, whatever it was, rob him of his joy. If he would no longer speak to her, she would simply scale up her effort, until he had to respond. The worship chamber, Chavah knew, was very close to the heart of Solomon. If she presented him a gift there, he would surely respond.

******

Solomon sat in his seat behind the bench of the judgment hall, where he was recording some final notes after a day of hearing testimony and rendering judgments. He was obsessed with justice, and nothing drew harder on his compassion than oppression of the poor. His eyes never failed to seek out the downcast, and he could identify an oppressed person in a crowd almost by the expression on their face. But the last case of the day left a bad taste in his mouth because a man called Asa-Barak, whom Solomon was sure was guilty of murder, had escaped a verdict. Solomon had tried a ruse to coax a conflicting story out of the man, but had botched the order of his questions, allowing the man to see the trap just in time. Solomon was bound by the law to send the criminal to the city of refuge—an unsolved case. It was the first case in over two hundred that had gone that way. He worried that his all-consuming personal issues were beginning to affect his work.

It had been a bad day to begin with. With concern over his lack of a queen pressing upon him constantly, he had summoned Naamah for a tour of the Temple grounds in hope—though a distant one—that more direct exposure would inspire in her some passion for the Israelite religion. True, the prospect of putting forth this Ammonitess as queen was fraught with political challenges, but with few other options in sight, he designed to give Naamah every opportunity to rise to it. Perhaps, this time, the faith of the Israelites would finally take root in her. Then her brave mind could assist him in navigating the politics of bringing her into the position of queen.

Solomon had not actually taken her into the Temple—that would have been unthinkable—but he did stroll with her upon the wall, attempting to engage her in conversation while pointing to its various features.

Naamah, he quickly discovered, was angry, and more deeply than he knew. Naamah's anger was not like that of other women, a storm that blew in, spent its fury, and disappeared. Her anger was intelligent—and lasting. It found its way to the surface through stilted comments and barely discernible sarcasm. She met his overtures concerning the Temple with well-stated and perfect responses, revealing a very complete understanding of the technicalities of Israelite worship—so complete, in fact, that it was entirely without soul, the product of a mind that had laboriously committed to memory things in which it had no natural interest.

While Solomon continued to search for a way to pique Naamah's curiosity, she used the rare opportunity to draw his attention to her own complaints: her abode outside of the city and the plight of the Ammonite people. Letters from the homeland continued to insist, she said, that Ammonites were being abused in the king's labor force. This very Temple, with which Solomon was so enraptured, was, she said, to blame for the whole atrocity. She could see in it nothing but oppression. His comments on the cutting and fitting of the stones were met with complaints about who carried them. Solomon and Naamah had parted ways in a disagreeable silence—Solomon in grief, Naamah in the cold calculation of revenge.

The unhappy memory of this exchange pooled with the unsatisfactory result of the final case of the day, forming a bitter brew in his soul as Solomon sat behind the judgment bench recording notes.

He looked up. The still outline of a woman was in the far doorway.

Chavah.

Chavah was not often found standing statuesque, as she was just now, having the habit, rather, of always scurrying off to or from some amusement. Solomon rose, regarding curiously the beautiful woman silhouetted against the bright background. Had something happened? Had the Lord finally spoken to her?

"Chavah," he said.

She was silent. That also was odd. He descended from the bench and made his way down the central aisle to meet her. Her face was pregnant with meaning untold.

"I thought I might find you here," she said, purely serious

with not a hint of a smile, an expression he found strangely refreshing, contrasted as it was against her recent, almost desperate attempts to amuse him.

"What is it, love?"

Chavah looked at him poignantly.

"There is something I must tell you. I have known that I must tell you this for some time but have not had the courage. It is well known that you have been diverted in recent days, and I know the cause."

He studied her, cocking his head to one side, even as his pulse quickened.

"Truly?"

"Me," she continued. "I have failed you, and I have none to blame but myself."

Solomon swallowed.

"Is that so, my love? How do you mean?"

Finally she moved, stepping in through the doorway to stand closer to him, studying his eyes sincerely.

"I have known what a queen must be . . . what a queen must do, the sacrifices she must make for her king and his kingdom. But until now, I have not been willing to make them. I have been in your presence, but I have not ventured near your heart, even when I knew the way. I should bring you joy, but instead I bring you pain. I alone have allowed you to descend into the bleakness that your soul now experiences, when I had the power to prevent it. This should never be—not between us. We have been friends too long. I have failed you miserably."

"Chavah . . ."

"I intend to make it up to you, if you will allow me."

Hearing now words he had longed to hear for so long, he felt nothing but the urge to console, to insist that her failing was truly not so bad. But he knew truth would not allow such a consolation.

"Chavah, you have been . . . we have been friends, and there is nothing between us that we can not amend."

"Which is exactly why I have come," she replied. "Will you walk with me?"

A wave of compassion for her washed over him.

"Of course," he said, stepping forward. She turned and went back out the door, and he came up beside her, extending his arm for her to take, which she did.

"I have something to show you," she said, "a token of my repentance, that you may know my heart is attuned to yours."

He glanced at her curiously. There was still no hint of joviality in her demeanor.

"Come with me."

She indicated the pathway before them which wound among several gardens and palace buildings toward the site of the home under construction. After a peaceful walk of several minutes, they arrived at the entrance to the magnificent new house, and Chavah stopped. A vine had been planted to the right side of the main door, a vine which Chavah knew Solomon had taken an interest in—and even more so, since its health was questionable.

"That poor vine," she commented.

"Yes, it is disappointing."

"Has it enough water?"

"I have tended it myself—I do not know what more can be done for it."

She looked up at him with honest eyes.

"I am sorry."

He studied her.

"It is only a vine, my love; it is not important."

"Though in itself it is only a vine, its importance can not drop beneath that of the person to whom it matters," she replied.

He nodded, regarding her curiously. Not only was it a nice sentiment; it was, in fact, the most perceptive statement he had heard from her in a long time.

She met his studying eyes, perceiving his favor in them.

"I want to assure you that I am not blind to the deep pulses of your soul. That is why I am showing you what I have done here—that you may never doubt me again."

"Done?"

She smiled at him.

"Come." She took him by the hand and led him in through the door. He walked with her in silent curiosity as she made her way through the home, passing through several rooms in silence toward the center, where the worship chamber was situated. There she stopped in front of the door and turned her back to it to face him.

"I know this house is special to you, and no place in it more special than this room."

He was nodding. Did she finally truly understand?

"And so it is here where I have chosen to show you my repentance. I have a gift for you, and I can only give it to you here."

He studied her intently, his apprehension growing.

"Chavah? What have you done?"

"Only my very best. And you alone are worthy of it. I give you all my very best, my best work, the fruit of my life."

"Chavah . . ."

She put her hand on the door and slowly pushed it open, allowing him to enter. Solomon stepped forward, tentatively, into the room. Suddenly he gasped, his eyes roaming up and around widely and wildly.

"Oh," he whispered, putting his hand to his temple.

There, in the walls of the seven-sided worship chamber,

which contained the many empty cases—cases which had been both sized and designed to represent years of worship of Jehovah through the seven feasts and holy days of the sacred Israelite calendar—there from within those very cases stared back at Solomon statues and sculptures in every available place: from top to bottom, in every corner. Every piece was hand-crafted artwork, made and placed by Chavah herself. Each was her unique handiwork and design, yet filled with the visible influences and shades of every foreign god known in the world. Could it possibly be?

"Chavah!" he whispered in horror.

She stared at him, trying to discern his strange reaction.

"Chavah, what have you done?!"

Her face went flat.

"I . . . I . . . offer you . . ."

"Ichabod! Ichabod! Chavah, this sanctuary was created for worship—of Jehovah!—and you have defiled it with the filth of the nations!"

"Wor—worship?"

"Yes! Worship of the one true God! Chavah, these are idols!"

She looked up, examining her artwork in puzzlement.

"They are not idols," she whispered. "It is just art. Does not all art belong to God?"

He gasped, perplexed.

"Art?! Chavah! Do you not know that spirits attach themselves to certain kinds of art? Do you not know that the heathen venerate these images as their gods? God made all art, to be sure, but Belial twists it, defiling it by his filthy worship, and as long as men associate these things with Belial, it is for us unclean. Unclean! An abomination of the worst kind! Chavah, how could you do this?!! Have you lost all sense? How could you?!"

He stared down at her wildly.

She took a step back from him in fear, placing her hand over

84

her chest, never before having seen such a reaction from her gentle king.

"I . . . I . . . I . . ." she stammered.

Staring at her, Solomon let out a loud groan that was something beyond words. It echoed up into the high recesses of the chamber. He leaned toward her almost imperceptibly, then grabbed his robes in the front and tore them violently in two—the Hebrew gesture of great sorrow.

Looking into his crazed pupils, Chavah was suddenly afraid of him. He turned, abruptly and violently, crashed into a wall, rebounded toward the door, and stumbled out. She stepped after him and called. "Solomon!"

"Silence! Away from me!"

He staggered toward the door of the house, stumbling out into a run. He cleared the threshold, blurry-eyed with grief and awe at what he had just seen, and stumbled blindly back down the path along which they had just come, back toward the palace. Passing before the curious eyes of palace personnel, the king labored up the stairs to his chamber and slammed the door, pulling down the locking crossbeam.

Chavah had followed him for a few steps and then resigned to let him go, looking in the direction he had gone, and then eventually wandering back to the worship chamber to stare up in confusion at the collection of her most carefully crafted works elegantly displayed in the room's many cases. She shook her head in bafflement and teared up. Finally, she slammed the door to the chamber in rage, causing everything in the room to shake, and stomped out the main door, slamming it in like fashion.

****

The morning was bright, but ominous. Bathsheba quickened her pace yet again as she hastened toward the royal stable where Solomon's personal livestock was kept. She hoped she was not too late. If not for the fact that she had been informed by a palace aide that something unusual was taking place, Solomon would have slipped away without her knowing. But now the palace was abuzz with the news: The young king Solomon had called for an emergency meeting with his top advisors and had hastily set affairs in order to allow himself an unexplained "leave of absence." Something was wrong.

As Bathsheba rounded the back of the palace building, her eyes leaped ahead across the wide stone courtyard used for the staging of chariots and, with some relief, recognized the familiar forms of the guards, Jachin and Boaz, near the stable door.

They will not be far from him.

She had sent messengers to call for Nathan the prophet, but Solomon was acting so quickly and decisively that she doubted he would arrive before her son had departed, leaving her to try to reason with him herself.

Presently, Jachin emerged through the stable door into which he had disappeared moments earlier, leading a fine stallion, and two servants helped to hoist and tie a pack onto the animal. A moment later, Bathsheba recognized the unmistakable profile of her son as he emerged leading Shishak, his own favorite stallion, a stunning white Arabian that had come from Pharaoh's most elite stock. She gushed a sigh of relief at the sight of him, even as she quickened her pace once again. Solomon looked up to see his mother as she made her way toward him as fast as her age and her garments would allow. She lifted her arm in a wave to catch his eye, as though such a gesture could detain him a few moments longer.

Solomon turned around and gave instructions to another pair of servants as they loaded his horse with a travel pack, then pointed back into the stable as he gave still more directions to others.

"Solomon!" Bathsheba cried as she came up to them. He turned to face his mother, and when he did, she saw a most odd expression on his face. She recognized it as a highly disciplined façade covering deep distress. His features were gaunt beneath his bushy beard, which had grown quite shaggy in recent weeks, and he looked very tired, as if he had not slept at all the previous night. The truth was, he hadn't. He managed a polite smile and forced a calm casualness in his voice as he greeted her with the formal "Blessings, Mother."

"Solomon!" she exclaimed with greater desperation in her tone, even as her voice lowered in volume. "I heard you had come down here. The reports in the palace are that you are leaving?" she ended with a question.

Solomon turned to give more instructions to his aides, then straightened himself to face her.

"You would leave without telling me?" she asked, searching his eyes. They seemed far away. She chanced a glance at his two guards, who revealed by silently catching her eye that they, too, were distraught at the present turn of events.

"I have a bit of business to attend to," Solomon said simply.

"Business? But where? How long? Just the three of you?"

"I go to see Huram-Abi," he said.

The friendship that had developed between Solomon and the prince from Tyre, the incomparably skilled craftsman who was overseeing the construction of the Temple, was legendary. Huram, a most uncommon and intelligent man, had won the trust of Solomon as few men could. He was one of a rare group that could meet the king mind for mind, at least in his own field of expertise. Huram had been gone from Jerusalem for some time to inspect another raft of logs from Tyre before export, and to approve a new quarry for additional stones.

Bathsheba looked around at the evidence of her son's imminent departure, not knowing quite how to react to his painfully brief and unsatisfying explanation. Her advisors had been right: The king would explain his actions to no one.

"But, son, is it not unsafe to travel alone like this? Can not messengers be sent to Huram-Abi?"

Solomon pursed his lips as he studied her. Of all the advantages a king enjoyed, he had one decided disadvantage: He could do nothing in private. His every word and action was subjected to constant examination, a ruthless and persistent examination, imaginative observers tagging the most mundane of actions with political intrigue. His plan for a hasty departure was his best attempt at circumventing the phenomenon—to be gone before many questions could be asked, questions he could not answer. Following the incident with Chavah the previous night, his urge had been dangerously close to a desire to flee. He had finessed it into something more acceptable: a temporary hiatus from responsibility, where he could put his full focus on the most difficult problem he had yet encountered as king. Still, a little voice told him he was running.

So be it!

No advisor could help him now. The cases at the judgment bar, no matter how complex, held no comparison to this, for this issue pierced his very soul. Justice demanded that his own heart now be probed, the sharp scalpel of spiritual examination poking at its most sensitive places. The bright light of discernment must now shine directly upon the excruciating conflict between himself and his presumed queen-to-be. Like an animal wishing to suffer alone, he set his face away. What to other men would have been a private matter, was for him the pressing business of the kingdom. The issue had to be faced, in all of its agony. And that, he could only do alone.

"Mother," he explained, discerning her desperation, "we will be traveling the high country, not the main roads. You know well the protection of Jachin and Boaz. Even if we do encounter anyone, it is highly unlikely that I will even be recognized," he said, opening his arms, palms up, before him.

She looked him over. He had in fact traded his royal garments for something much more drab and common-looking. She had to agree with him. With his shaggy beard and gaunt expression, he looked more like a beggar than a king. Outside of Jerusalem, the vast majority of Israelites had never even seen him up close. Removed from his royal entourage and traveling in a small band, it was quite likely he could go completely unnoticed.

"Son, I know something is wrong. Something you are not saying. It is Chavah, isn't it?"

At the sound of her name, he froze for a split second, then blinked and turned away from his mother, gaining emotional space through the feigned helping of a servant to cinch up the pack on his horse. Jachin and Boaz exchanged a glance upon hearing the queen's name spoken aloud.

"After meeting Huram-Abi, we will be traveling on to Lebanon," Solomon said.

Bathsheba knew her son was extremely fond of the high and wild beauty of Lebanon, as his father David had been. As a boy, Solomon had hiked the hills of Amana, and always seemed to enjoy a spiritual renaissance in that place. Discerning that her son was not going to be deterred from his course, Bathsheba quickly rearranged her goals toward gaining as much information as possible.

"I do wish you would take some time to plan and prepare before rushing off like this. The kingdom can not be left unattended for long. When can we expect your return?"

"I will be back in time for Yom Kippur. My counselors have been advised," he replied.

Bathsheba gaped, but only inwardly. Yom Kippur! The fall feast was over two months away!

"But, son, so long! How can the kingdom manage such an absence? There is business that must . . ."

"The kingdom has no greater business than for its king to resolve this matter."

The voice came from near the stable. All heads turned to see the prophet Nathan, holding his staff, leaning against the wall as though he had been there all day. How long had he been there? All eyes were now on Nathan, but the prophet's eyes focused only on the eyes of the king. The two stared at each other in a long moment of silence. Then, inexplicably, the prophet moved, took up his staff, and disappeared, shuffling around the corner.

The moments that followed were of a most awkward silence. The three horses had been fully prepared and were now stomping and swishing their tails in the mid-morning sun, which suddenly seemed exceedingly bright, while the servants who had been assisting now stood nearby awaiting further instructions.

"The prophet has spoken," Solomon said into the air, addressing no one in particular, and then bent his head down toward his mother.

Her eyes welled as he leaned down to kiss her cheek. Then he turned and, with some vigor, swung up onto his horse. He looked at his two guards, who interpreted the silent command and hastily mounted also.

"We will exit through the back gate, follow the canal to the shepherd's gate, and then head east toward the hill road through Judea, above the Jordan valley," Solomon explained. "With the help of the Lord, we will be out of the city without notice."

He looked back around at his mother, who was staring up at him with fearful, tear-filled eyes.

"Do not be afraid," he said.

Then he looked decidedly away and spurred his horse forward.

Bathsheba scurried after them for a few steps.

"Be careful, my son!" He glanced back at her and nodded.

"I love you!" she said.

He turned again and bowed slightly with his head, mouthing the words back to her. Then she was left, powerlessly watching her beloved son and his two guards ride across the courtyard toward the back gate where he would disappear—perhaps, as a mother's heart is always prone to fear . . . forever.

Know you my language? I the Dove cooed to the Frog.
The frog was cross with me. He frowned and kicked and splashed.
I went away sad.

Know you my language? I cooed to the Flower.
It smiled at me.
My heart leapt!
I waited long, but the flower said nothing.
I went away sad.

Know you my language? I cooed to one who flew like I.
It spoke back to me!
I spoke of something else, but it did not understand me.
It kept repeating the same thing.
I went away sad.

I saw my reflection, but there was no pool.
Know you my language? I cooed to it.
It cooed back, and spoke of something else.
I understood, and cooed again!
It spoke back again!
And so it went.
From that time, I was happy.

Chapter 8

He that oppresseth the poor reproacheth his Maker: but he that honoureth him hath mercy on the poor.

—Proverbs 14:31

Solomon lay in his brushy recline at the bottom of the ravine. As the moon began to rise, he held his stomach and shivered against the memory pangs, then finally dozed off into a fitful half-sleep. The misty autumn dew came in like a cruel handmaid and dropped a cold, wet blanket over his outer clothing.

Surely Jachin and Boaz will find me soon.

But Solomon's guards were not as near as he supposed. Upon returning to camp and finding him missing, they had first scoured the nearby area to no avail. In growing panic they returned to camp and tried to discern the trail by which their king had left. However, they seized upon the wrong trail, one which led to the far side of the mountain, where they were even now combing the wilderness in a desperate search.

Meanwhile, Solomon roused, awakened by the unexpected sound of music—angels, the singing of angels—or . . . or . . . Just where was he, anyway?

He looked up at the starry sky and remembered. The Orion

had moved west, out of his immediate vision. The harvest moon was about a quarter of the way up the sky. That meant perhaps an hour had passed. But what was that sound? Footsteps . . . singing . . . Why, it was a woman, passing not ten cubits from him! Apparently he had fallen near a path that circled around the base of the ridge. He strained and looked around behind himself to see a dark form moving down the trail away from where he lay, the music of her humming fading off into the night. He could see she was carrying a large basket balanced on her head. He squinted through the brush and noticed the silhouettes of some carefully placed posts and vines. A vineyard. The woman continued down the path.

He thought, *Probably a laborer or a slave, coming in late from a day of harvesting.*

Suddenly, there was a shout, the sound of a commotion, and the voice of an angry man down the path.

"Such trash as this, look what your bleeding-heart ways have brought upon us!"

The woman's response was soft and indiscernible.

Then a child's voice broke in. "Please, I did not know I was in your vineyard. I thought I was in hers."

"I warned you about this!" shouted the man. "You let one of them in, and next thing you know, the whole country is overrun with them! Look at this, there's probably a bekah-and-a-half worth of grapes you have there, you scurvy little thief!"

"Ouch, let go of me!" screamed the child.

"Now that's enough, Barkos!" shouted the woman. "Let her go!"

"No! Who is going to pay for this? I ought to tie you up and throw you in the swamp, you worthless little waif! This is private property, and we will not tolerate . . ."

The child began to cry.

"Look!" exclaimed the woman. "I have more than enough here to replace what she has taken! For all the grapes she has in that little basket you can take double from what I have here! Don't you realize that the only reason the ground produces fruit for us at all is because we honor the One who created it? The Law of Moses allows the orphan and widow to glean. Disregard the laws of God and you will see this whole valley turned into a desert!"

"Listen! I'm not King Solomon here, woman! I just have one little patch of ground, that's all I got, and it's barely enough to live on. You quote the Law to me? I'll give you some law! That's my landmark right there, this is my land, this was my father's land, and anyone who wants any fruit can get it at the market tomorrow morning, as long as they show the money to pay for it!" he yelled.

The woman responded softly. "Do not rob the poor because he is poor, nor oppress the afflicted at the gate, for the Lord will plead their cause, and plunder the soul of those who plunder them. And that is not the Law; those are the words of King Solomon."

Solomon's eyebrows went up in curiosity at her mention of his name. He leaned around, trying to get a better view through the brush, surprised to hear his own words correctly quoted in such a remote place.

"When King Solomon sees what I have to deal with, then maybe he'll have something to say to me," the man seethed. "Until then, it's far too easy for him to sit up there in his plush palace and spout proverbs. Now, give me my fruit back!"

"My lord, would it be all right with you if you took my fruit, too?" asked the woman. "Here, take it; it's yours—and all the profit from it. And anyone else you find gleaning here by mistake, you just come to me, and I'll replace double for what you have lost. I will not have orphaned children going hungry in this land of abundance with which God has blessed us!"

"All right, you got yourself a deal, woman!"

There were a few moments of silence as the man stomped off.

Then the woman called out loudly, "And the only reason

Solomon has anything at all is because he is a man who honors the God of Israel!"

Her words echoed off the hills and hung in the quiet night air, drawing no response. Then she began to speak softly, comforting the whimpering child. Solomon leaned forward, straining to hear and to get a better look. After a few moments, the woman and child disappeared back down the path.

Solomon rolled back onto his back and stared up into the sky again. The majestic form of an eagle passed into his view in a long, slow circle. Then, he saw it joined by a second, tracing the same circle of flight. For a long time, the final words of the woman rang in his ears. Finally, he fell asleep again and soon found himself in the grip of a strange and unsettling dream.

He was traveling somewhere on urgent business, feeling the weight of responsibility and desperate to get to his destination. He was walking alone down a mountain road with no map to guide him. All at once, he came to a place where many roads crossed. There were no signs or markings of any kind to tell him which to take. Desperate to continue toward his destination, he knelt before the Lord and asked him which road to follow. Not receiving any discernible answer, he set out in what appeared to be the general direction he needed to go. After a short while, the road dead-ended at a little provincial farm. Not even a farm, really—just a little peasant dwelling, with a mud hut for a house, a couple of animal buildings, some fruit trees, and what looked like a small guest hut. He did not recognize the place. Frustrated, he hurried back to the crossroads and took another path, only to find himself arriving at the same place again, but coming at it from a different angle. The road that had existed the last time he was here . . . was gone! He had to return by the way he had come.

And so it repeated, on and on: No matter which road he took, he ended up at the same place. In growing desperation, he knelt in the middle of the crossroads again, pleading with the Lord to help him find his way. When he opened his eyes, he felt something in his hand. Looking down, he saw a scrap of paper on which he read the words, "... *return now to the place of beginnings, to the east ...*"

Solomon frowned at the strange words. Then he caught

something out of the corner of his eye and turned to see a sign, partially obscured in the bushes by the roadside. It had been there all along, but he had not noticed it before. He rushed forward and cleared the branches away. On the sign were printed these simple words: *"A man's heart plans his way, but the LORD directs his steps."*

Eventually, the dream faded into mist as the approaching morning coaxed him to consciousness. The emotions of the dream lingered in his soul, leaving a strange and ominous imprint.

Solomon opened his eyes. The morning birds were in full chorus, and the nearby plants sparkled with dew. The sun was up but not yet visible over the ridge to the east. His whole body was stiff and cold. He rolled up into a sitting position and scanned the terrain around him. What had been mysterious shadows in the dark of night revealed themselves as common, simple things in the daylight: a rock, a tree, the profile of a hill. He was near the uppermost section of a vineyard that stretched up the hill, beyond which it was too steep to plant. From where he sat, across the path he could see the dark ripe fruit on the vines. His mouth watered. He leaned forward and started to stand, but gasped as sharp pain in his ankle forced him immediately to find support against a large rock.

He also noticed a flurry of various aches and pains from his bruises—or was it from his awkward sleep? Judging by the tightness of his boot leather against his foot, he realized his foot must be quite swollen. He looked up and around, trying to see over the vineyard. There were probably homes nearby, but he could not see any. There was nothing to do but try to walk.

Gingerly, he limped across the path and leaned on a post that supported a frame on which the vines grew. To brace himself further, he placed his hands on the two large, earthen water pots that stood on either side of the post. Each movement revealed a new ache, and he realized he could put hardly any weight at all on his foot.

Solomon reached up and picked a cluster of grapes. They looked delicious. From where he stood, he harvested as many as he could reach, tucking them into a fold of his clothing. Then he slumped down against the post and was about to partake when he remembered his Nazarite vow—no fruit of the vine was allowed, whether fresh, dried, or in the form of wine. Solomon groaned, looking at the delicious, ripe clusters, his mouth watering for them.

When this is all over, I ought to buy a vineyard out here.

The sun was rising behind the rock and promising to burst out upon him soon. *That will be nice*, he thought, shivering. He limped back across the trail, then realized the rock he had been leaning on was actually the stone rim of a well. As he sat down on its edge, something caught his eye. He peered up the path to see a woman walking his way, carrying a large basket. She topped a rise and disappeared into a draw. A few moments later, he could hear her footsteps coming up the next rise toward him. She was humming, and Solomon recognized the tune he had heard the night before. Then she appeared over the rise, fully covered from head to toe in the manner of a virgin, in a plain laborer's tunic of drab gray, un-dyed wool. Merrily, she came marching up the path.

"Shalom," he said.

Startled, the woman turned toward him.

"Shalom."

He looked at her. She looked at him. Her eyes peered out of her veil, the only part of her visible to interact with. A peasant girl, dressed for a day of work in the field. He stared back from under his turban. He saw her eyes travel down, scanning his appearance and clothing. He glanced down. He had been dressed for the mountains. There was nothing about his attire that would reveal royalty.

"You know, if you want to glean here, you may want to come up the path a bit. This is Barkos's vineyard, and he allows no gleaning here," she said.

"So I have heard. I fell from that ridge over there and spent the night in that bush."

She regarded him warily.

"So . . . you heard what happened last night."

98

"Yes, I did."

"And still you glean here?"

"I am not gleaning. I have money to pay for what I have taken."

She looked him over again, scanning his clothing. It was torn and dirty, damp with dew. With his unshaven face and the long, stringy locks of his Nazarite vow creeping down his neck, he probably looked to her like a homeless, penniless vagabond.

"Well, that being the case, my lord," she said, "I would just as soon have you pay *me* then. Please, my lord, come down the path to glean; you can pay me next time you travel this way."

"You are very kind, daughter, but I have no wish to buy fruit. But neither am I gleaning, I am traveling. Does not the law of Moses allow the passing traveler to pick from the fields what his hands can hold, as long as he does not collect it into any bowl or basket?"

The woman pursed her lips skeptically. That was the only Law of Moses that drifters such as this could quote.

"Besides which, I do not know if I can walk," he continued. "I hurt my ankle when I fell off that ridge last night."

Her countenance grew serious.

"You are injured, my lord?"

"Yes. But not too badly, I think."

Her eyes traveled down.

"May I examine your ankle?"

He studied her thoughtfully. He *did* need help.

"If you would be so kind. You are aware that if your neighbor's ox stumbles, you shall certainly not walk by. How much more a man? For it is not oxen that God is concerned about, but men."

She glanced into his eyes, then set down her basket. This particular vagabond knew the Law a bit better than most. And she

99

was beginning to notice a certain polish in his speech and manners. He leaned back over the well and stretched out his leg. Then he pulled up his robe to reveal his feet, immaculately clad in long, black leather boots. She stepped forward and peered at them curiously. He noticed her skeptical expression.

"And the hand of a thief is to be cut off?" he offered, tossing out a common misquote.

"That is not in the Law of Moses."

"Neither am I a thief."

She sighed. "Well, then . . . whoever you are . . . let's have a look at that ankle."

She knelt down and gently felt his ankle with her hands. He looked down at her veiled head. There was something strangely familiar about her, but he could not quite place it.

"Anyway," she mumbled, glancing up at him, "these boots are more of a problem now."

He chuckled. He also got a good look at her eyes for the first time. They were quite striking, for a peasant girl, large and dark.

"Don't worry—I have others. And you do know my name," he said.

"I beg your pardon?"

"You already said it once."

"Hmm?"

"Did you not walk up here and bid me 'Shalom' a moment ago?" he asked.

"'Shalom' is your name?"

"The sense of it. What is your name?"

She continued carefully feeling around his puffy ankle.

"Well, I've got bad news for you, my lord. You're not going to get this boot off without a knife. Your ankle is so swollen, you won't possibly be able to pull it out." She eyed him, expecting to see some remorse at the destruction of the boot.

"A knife I have," Solomon said, reaching into his belt and producing an instrument with a beautiful blade, marble handle, gold stop, and diamond-studded end cap. Spinning it expertly in his hand, he held the handle toward her. Her eyes went wide.

"And don't worry. As I said, I have other boots, too."

She gingerly took the knife out of his hand.

"Who are you?" she asked, genuinely puzzled now.

"I told you my name, but you did not tell me yours."

"My lord, I am a virgin. If you wish to speak to me by name, you must address my father first."

"Who is your father?"

"My father is dead."

"Well, that will keep you safely anonymous for life," he quipped.

She was silent for a moment, carefully working the knife down the stitches of his boot. Was she actually trying to save the boot?! Then he heard her sniff.

"I'm sorry," he said. "I didn't know you . . ."

"No, it's all right," she said, calmly wiping a tear from her cheek. "It was a long time ago. I am the only one of my mother."

"So that's how a peasant girl comes to be the owner of such a fine vineyard."

"Well, technically, it belongs to my brothers—half-brothers. My father also had an Egyptian wife."

"And your mother was an Israelite?"

"Yes. My father wanted an Israelite son to be his heir. Instead, they got me. My brothers never forgot and, to this day, deny that I am the daughter of their father, for if I should marry, they are afraid that this vineyard, and everything else my father owned, would be taken from them. I work this vineyard since it is the only support my brothers have allotted for my mother. Everything else they have kept for themselves. They will not

101

maintain it. If I did not maintain it, it would become a jungle in one season. But their own mother lives like a queen." She stopped short, suddenly embarrassed that she had said so much to a total stranger.

Solomon chuckled.

"You do not know how a queen lives."

"And you do?"

He glanced at her thoughtfully.

"Would your half-brothers lose the inheritance if you were to marry?" he asked, probing her knowledge of the Law on a rather arcane point.

"That depends whom you ask," she said.

"I am asking you."

She sighed.

"I am no rabbi, my lord," she answered, but he saw in her eyes that she did know the answer.

"Well, then, you won't lose any respect if you get it wrong then, will you?"

She stopped and looked up at him. Then she declared firmly, "If I marry, and the man is an Israelite, he has an inheritance of his own, so there is no risk to them. If I marry a non-Israelite, he has no inheritance here, so again there is no risk."

"Well said. Yet, they still worry?"

"Yes."

"Why?"

"Because the Law, to them, is like a metal rod. It has been twisted so far, so often, that they do not know anymore which way is straight."

"Hmm," Solomon responded, eyebrows going up. "May I have permission to quote you?"

She looked up at him in surprise.

"I have occasion to comment on the Law from time to time," he explained.

She sighed. "If the uncensored ramblings of an ignorant peasant girl could ever be of such noble use, I would be the last person to object. But I confess I find the likelihood of such a thing laughably remote."

Solomon looked at her anew. Her answer sounded as little like the "ramblings of an ignorant peasant girl" in eloquence as it did in unaffected humility.

"A wise statement recommends itself, dear maiden," he replied carefully, "and the station of its source cannot detract from it."

She blushed.

"In any case, I merely intended to note that you do seem to know something of the Law," he added.

"Yes, well, perhaps I'm just too innocent to know any better than just to take it for what it says. You see, Baal Hamon owns most of the land around here, even though he is no Israelite. He did not obtain it by following the Law, but by making the Law follow him. My brothers have seen this happen so many times they have no confidence in the Law. My brothers are not Israelites either, at least according to Baal Hamon, so they play by his rules."

"Which are?"

"Which are: See things his way, and he will let you keep what you have. Stir the kettle, and you may lose everything."

"And your marrying would stir the kettle?"

She continued staring at the boot as she worked the knife farther down the stitches.

"You have a lot of questions, don't you? It is simply a matter of how it would appear. Yes, my marrying would raise uncomfortable questions. That, or if my other brother were to return."

"So, your father did have an Israelite son for an heir then."

She sighed. This man seemed to cut to the heart of things quickly.

"Frankly, my lord, I do not know if he was Israelite or not. He left before I was born, and I have never met him. I will find out if and when he returns."

Solomon considered for a moment. It was a most interesting situation, and this simple conversation with the peasant girl was offering him a unique perspective on life in rural Israel. He usually heard such cases while sitting in the judgment seat where every argument raised was heavily stacked. This kind of casual conversation was rare for him. He decided to keep the moment alive, just for the sake of finding out what else of value he might learn from it.

"You have never seen your brother? Never in your life?" he asked.

"No, never, and when he comes, I have some questions for him."

Solomon's mind whirled and lit on a daring idea.

"Well, then, ask," he blurted, not quite sure why he had just said that.

She froze, looking up at him hard, as though trying to look right through him.

"Ahh," he said. "And, how will you know it is he?"

She continued to stare at him.

Solomon smiled at her. She studied his face, trying to see what it might reveal. He was well seasoned from his years on the judgment seat to reveal nothing with his face. He waited, but so did she. She was not going to speak next.

"Well, then," he said, "am I to gather that you have lived your whole life in expectation of the return of a long-lost brother, but you never stopped to consider how you would know him when you saw him?"

"But . . . my mother . . ." she began, realizing right away that after so many years, her mother would not recognize him either. "Well," she said finally, "I guess I just supposed he would introduce himself."

"Mmmm," Solomon responded. "And just how would he know *you*?"

She was silent.

"There is many a man who could be your brother if he were to find out there was a fine vineyard in it for him," Solomon warned.

She remained quiet. He waited.

Finally, she looked up firmly. "I do not like this game, my lord. It seems to me that you ask me what you alone can answer. My true brother, seeking me out with honest intentions, would have the advantage of forethought. With an estate hanging in the balance, he certainly would have foreseen this moment, and would come with proof. The onus is on you, my lord. If you are truly my brother, you tell me: How do I know it?"

Solomon hesitated in a rare moment of indecision. It was the perfect answer! She held his gaze in silence, then returned to working on the boot.

Solomon's mind sped ahead, trying to locate an answer quickly. If, in fact, he were her brother and knew where to come to find her, he would also know other things—things about her, perhaps some family secrets, things that could prove his identity to her. This little peasant girl had all but broken his ruse in a moment. He inhaled to speak, but then yelped in pain as the boot suddenly slipped off his foot with a lurch.

The woman looked up to see him grimacing, his pupils dilating with the pain, eyes tearing up. Yet, he cried out only the once. She winced as well to see him suffering, though he now displayed immense control. Not a common trait in a beggar.

"My lord, I am afraid your ankle is broken," she said.

Solomon nodded vigorously in agreement.

Then a thin line of blood appeared on his ankle where the seam of the boot had been. Soon it flowed freely down his leg and off his foot.

"Oh, my soul!" the woman cried. "Look what I have done! I am so sorry! I've cut you! Oh, I am so clumsy!" She began to cry, looking all around for a cloth or something—anything—to use on the wound.

"Forgive my immodesty, please," she said finally as she removed the part of her veil that went over her head and bent down to wrap his foot in it. As she did, a splendid head of flowing hair, black and shiny as a raven, was released like a waterfall. Her tears dropped down onto his feet, mixing with the blood, as her hands worked quickly to get the scarf around behind the heel. Her long, wavy locks hung down onto the front of his foot, getting mixed in the blood and tears. She bundled a shiny lock of hair into one hand and used it to wipe up the bloody mixture, quickly bringing the scarf around to the front of his foot. Then she wrapped the scarf, gently but tightly, several times around and up the ankle.

Solomon was absolutely stunned as he watched her perform with such sacrificial kindness for a complete stranger. Here he was—for all she knew, a homeless, destitute beggar or, worse, some kind of swindler—yet she was treating him like the king of the world. The tears welled up in Solomon's eyes, but not on account of the pain.

"I am so sorry, my lord," she said with deep sincerity, looking up at him honestly, unflinching. He looked down at her face with its large, brown eyes moistened with tears and its expression pure as a lily. He gazed upon her long, flowing hair and her neck like that of a fawn. Solomon was stunned—speechless! For a moment he forgot the pain in his foot. He had never seen a woman so lovely. And he realized at that moment why she was so familiar. He knew this girl!

When King David was old, and could no longer keep warm when sleeping, a search was made through the land for a lovely maiden to assist him, keep him warm, and tend to his needs. Abishag the Shunammite, was chosen. Solomon suddenly remembered his party had camped right above the village of Shunem, the night before. This, therefore, was certainly that very maiden.

Abishag had been deemed the loveliest virgin in all the kingdom. But it remained a rumor only, simply because she had never revealed her face; she always wore the virgin's veil, both for modesty and to prove that she was not a concubine to David. Abishag had gained a reputation about the palace for being untouchable. Solomon was one of a select few who had ever seen her without her face covering—that was at least five years ago, and never this directly. She would allow no man to get close to her. Only those who selected her as his father's nurse knew how lovely she truly was.

Solomon was certain, without a doubt, that this *was* Abishag. But would *she* recognize *him*?

He calculated quickly: She had certainly seen him before, but that would have been when he was barely more than a boy, and beardless. He would have gained at least four inches in height since then, and a fair amount of weight. He and Abishag had seldom been in close proximity, and even then, all the attention would have been on his father. He was certain she had never seen him out of his royal attire, and certainly never with long hair.

Slowly, he pulled back the turban that had been partially covering his face against the night mist. She continued to look at him, frowning just a touch, but saying nothing.

"Daughter," he said softly, "your apology is accepted, and your kindness is beyond measure. But it is really I who ought to be apologizing to you. I wanted to make sure it was you with whom I was speaking, and that is why I questioned you so. I meant no harm."

"My lord?" she asked.

Suddenly, Solomon said something surprising, even to himself.

"I have been to Jerusalem in search of you. I had expected to find you there, but when you were not found, this was the only other place I knew to come. Certain things were told me as a lad—your name, where my family was, where I might find you— and when you worked in the king's employ, the word reached my ears, and I went there in search of you." What was he doing?! It was as though he were hearing someone else speak.

Her eyes narrowed. "How do you know that? No one here knows that it was I, and only those in the king's house would have my name. Have you been to the king's house?"

"I have, and when I came to Jerusalem in search of you, they confirmed to me that you were alive. If I could speak your name to you, would you find it convincing?"

"Say it," she breathed, her eyes wide with wonder.

"Abishag."

"Yes," she whispered.

For a maiden who had worn the virgin's veil since the first blush of womanhood, it was unprecedented for her to meet a stranger who could look at her face and declare to her her name. But still, his story did not make complete sense. It did not explain why he, if he were indeed her brother, would have known to look for her at the king's house. Her name had not been published.

She frowned. "I do not understand."

He, also, knew his story did not entirely add up, but he had certainly gained her attention. What to do now? He had waded in quite far—more so, in fact, than he had originally intended to, and he was not quite sure why. But he also felt compelled to continue . . . just a bit farther. Then he would reveal his identity. He looked down at her.

"Daughter, I am sorry if I have confused you. But certainly you would agree that, at the very least, we have some things to talk about. But at the moment, I am quite weary from an uncomfortable night, and if you please, I need to get somewhere where I can obtain care. Could you please go for help? A donkey would suffice."

"My lord, I have no donkey, but my home, and that of my

mother, is not far from here. Whether you are my brother or not, I would be honored to serve you there, if you can but walk a short space. And then, after you have rested, we will talk."

Solomon smiled. She smiled back.

"With your assistance, I can travel. Here, help me up," he said, reaching up with his hands.

"Yes, yes, of course," she said.

She took him by the arm. Carefully, he pulled himself up on his good leg, putting his arm around her shoulder. Together, they turned and faced the path. Then, slowly, they began working their way down the hill in the direction from which she had come. It was difficult going at first, and they had to keep the motion of their feet synchronized to make any good progress. Solomon winced in pain several times when their steps became disorganized and he briefly put weight onto his broken foot. But after a while, they found the necessary harmony.

There was not a lot of room for conversation in this awkward trip, but Solomon, in spite of his discomfort, could not help but notice the ravishing beauty of the woman by his side. She was truly stunning. He was certain no man had ever walked so closely with her for such a distance, and only under circumstances such as these would it have ever been possible. The richest, most powerful man in the world found himself feeling lucky to be here. No amount of money could have bought these affections from Abishag. They were not for sale.

Eventually, Solomon requested a moment to rest, and as they stood in the path, she supporting him, a man came upon them from behind.

"Shalom, Barkos," Abishag called out. "Are you going to the market soon?"

"Soon enough," he said curtly, looking curiously back and forth between the odd stranger and Abishag with part of her veil missing. "What is going on here?"

"Oh, yes, yes, of course," she said, remembering the need for introductions. "Barkos, this is . . . this is . . . um . . ."

"I am her brother," Solomon broke in.

She looked up at him searchingly.

"Brother?" Barkos asked. "Since when did you get another brother? Or should I say *a* brother?" he jabbed devilishly.

"I am not from around here," Solomon answered.

"He's not from around here," she echoed, knowing at least that much was true.

"I left my father's house at a young age, and now I am back to claim my inheritance," he continued.

Abishag didn't know quite how to behave. She did not want to deny his story, but neither could she affirm it, so she just stood by, looking nervous.

The man snorted. "Well, *brother*," he said mockingly, "I know a few other brothers who might have something to say about that!"

"That will be addressed at the proper time, but if you don't mind, my lord, we need to get home," he said.

"Hey, don't stop on my account," he said gruffly. "I got things to do here, too." He tromped on down the trail.

Meanwhile, Abishag's mother, Abelah, was in the farmyard going about her morning chores when she looked up and was taken aback at the strange sight on the path leading to her humble home. Two figures, strangely linked, one looking very much like her daughter, though partly unveiled, inched their way closer. Abelah quickly led the kid goats she was feeding back to their pen and scurried over to her mud hut. It appeared she was going to have a visitor, and she did not want to be an unprepared hostess. She put some bread that had been baked the day before, along with some goat cheese and grapes, onto the wooden crate she used for a table. Through the open door she could see the pair slowly making progress up the gentle rise into the yard. She could see now that the man was injured, and she hurried out to meet them.

When Solomon looked up from studying the ground, he

immediately recognized the place as the one in his dream!

"Shalom, my lord," Abelah said, bowing deeply before Solomon. "I see you are in need of assistance. Please come inside."

Solomon was perspiring hard from the pain and exertion of the walk. He could not respond, but looked eagerly toward the open door with relief upon his face. At long last they entered, and Solomon was carefully made to recline on a straw tick bed, a sackcloth pillow placed behind his head and his injured foot lifted to rest at last on a pile of blankets. He sighed deeply and, with eyes closed, spoke into the room.

"I thank you ever so kindly, dear woman, for your hospitality, and for the noble daughter that you have raised."

"You just rest now, my son," the widow said. "You've got some healing to do."

Something touched his hand. He opened his eyes and saw that Abishag was holding a cup of milk. He nodded and took the gift, drinking it down without stopping for a breath. Then he leaned back on the pillow and closed his eyes again.

Abishag watched as his fingers slowly relaxed on the cup. Just after he released it, but in the moment before it dropped, she deftly took it from his hand. Immediately, his breathing grew deep and steady.

Abishag crossed the room and stood before her mother, who looked up curiously.

"Mother!" she whispered. "Do you know who this is?"

"Who . . . who it is? Why, no. Do you?"

"Look at him—I mean, *really* look at him."

Abelah looked her guest over, up, down, face and clothing. Abishag watched her mother closely, her own face pensive with excitement.

"Abishag," Abelah said finally, "what do you see?"

Abishag proceeded to tell her about everything that had

111

happened, watching her mother's eyes grow wide when she told the part about his claiming to be her brother. From time to time, Abelah glanced over at the strange man in the corner.

"Tell me, Mother, the truth. Tell me about your other son. Tell me about my brother. What happened back then? How would we know him now, if he were to come to us?"

So that was it. The widow stared at her daughter in curious silence, then took a deep breath and walked over to the open doorway, staring out as if searching for something a great distance off.

"Abishag, I have never spoken with you about this out of respect for your father and for your brothers who are living. But now it appears the time has come. Your brother is not an Israelite. Before I was married to your father, I had another husband, who died—a Phoenician."

"Mother?" Abishag broke in.

"Yes. You see, in those days, we did not live here in Shunem. My family grew up in the land of the tribe of Naphtali, to the north, which borders what is now the land of Tyre. We were not a rich family, but my father worked the land. We survived, but with not much to spare. Then a famine came upon us, and my father fell into debt to a rich man, a craftsman from across the border, in Tyre. In order to recover his money, he was going to take our family's land. In those days, you understand, the land was sacred and the landmarks were still respected. My father would have sooner given the man his own two hands than to give up the inheritance of the Lord to a foreigner. So the man gave him another option: the hand of his daughter in marriage, as full payment."

"He sold you out?" Abishag gasped.

"No, daughter, no, he did not. Nor did he force me. I volunteered to go. The land of my family was all that we had. If I did not go, the loss would not just be mine, but my brothers would lose their inheritance forever. I had to go. The man was old—older than my father. I promised my father that when he died, I would come back to Israel and find a husband from among my own people, if possible, and be buried here in the Land of Promise."

She stopped speaking, staring out into space, lost in memories.

"What happened then?"

"Hmm? Oh, yes, well, in the course of time I became pregnant and gave him a son in his old age. He knew of the promise that I had made to my father, to return home, so he required that I make a promise to him, that his son would be raised in his own land. The boy was still very young when his father died, but his father was wealthy, had left an estate for him, and had paid for his career. He was to be trained as a craftsman, like his father, even from his tender youth. I had contacts who informed me of his progress for a time. He proved himself talented and became successful in the trade, as expected. I have heard no word of him for many years now, but if he carried any measure of his father's talents, he very likely became a great man in his field."

"That would explain his wealth," Abishag whispered to herself, remembering the fine boots and the expensive blade.

"Oh, certainly," the widow said. "There is every reason to expect his wealth would be great."

"Mother," Abishag said, leaning forward seriously, "what is his name?"

"His name?" the woman chuckled. "The name is not how you will know him, for his name is common. You must ask his father's name."

"What is that?"

"Fakhir-Bashshar Khalid," she declared, saying it reverently, as if it were an incantation.

"Fakhir-Bashshar Khalid," Abishag repeated, searching for a way to remember the regal-sounding name.

The two women looked back at their guest, still motionless in the corner, and silently considered the unique moment.

113

"Well, then that explains . . ." Abishag said, her mind putting things together. "If he is the son of a prince, that explains his access to the king's courts, why he would have had contacts there, where he could have heard about me and asked about me."

The older woman nodded. "Yes, I suppose it does, but what it does not explain is, how did he know your name, having been born before you?"

"Hmmm," Abishag replied, not finding an easy answer to this.

Neither did Solomon, who, it turned out, had been listening intently to every word. The Tyrean's name sounded faintly familiar to him. Where had he heard it before? His mind began tracing the royal genealogies he had memorized for the kingdom north of Israel. Where was that name found? It would come to him, he knew.

The situation was most interesting. With this new information, he believed he could continue with the role, if he so chose, for he could demonstrate all the necessary knowledge. But it raised another problem. It meant that his character was not an Israelite, at least not fully so, and had no right to claim an inheritance—and more than that, no *need* for one.

"Abishag," Abelah continued, "now that I have told you all of this, it is time to tell you something else. When my Tyrean husband died and I returned to Israel to marry again, I did not know until months later that the Lord had placed a second child in my womb."

"You lost him?"

Abelah smiled.

"No, I still have *her.*"

Abishag's mouth dropped open.

"I did not tell you because you were already so disrespected by your brothers. Since they were only half-Israelite, I wanted you to have the advantage of being considered a full Israelite. But, no, you are of that Tyrean father."

Solomon listened, but at the same time, his mind probed the other question, the one he could not quite answer, not even to himself—the question of why. Why was he doing this?

As mother and daughter continued to talk things over, his mind wandered. He thought about Chavah, and the great tragedy that had become of her. He thought of the kings of Egypt and Ammon, and the wives they had sent him. He thought about the daughters of Jerusalem, and how they continually fawned over him so. He thought of his need for a queen and an heir to the kingdom, and the stark vacancy left by Chavah's fall. For as long as he could remember, his future queen had been known to him. It was a given in life, just like the fact that he would one day be king. But now he was suddenly in desperate need of a queen.

Solomon found himself totally unprepared for such a surprising turn of events. How does one go about finding a queen, when she who has been chosen for you is disqualified?

I suppose, you must fill the position wisely, just like any other position in your kingdom. What kind of woman makes a good queen?

Then he considered Abishag: her beauty, her nobility, and her chastity. She was a unique person, at the very least. He also became aware, that for the short time he had spent with her, the blanket of sorrow which threatened to consume him had lifted. Even the soft rhythm of her voice across the room right now was soothing to his ears. She had treated him like a king even though she did not know he was one. Could this peasant girl have the makings of a queen? He turned the thought over in his mind.

But then, the revelation about her birth—she was not fully Israelite. How could it be possible that the Lord desired him to take a Gentile bride as queen? It was a most surprising thought, but, under the circumstances, he could not dismiss it. It was clear the Lord had led him here for some reason. Aside from the question of her ethnicity, how could he determine Abishag's fitness for the role? It would require careful consideration. It would require talking with her. Not just knowing *about* her, but knowing her heart as well. That would take time, and careful observation. Given the chance to examine her, he knew he would be able to determine if she was really as special as she seemed.

And what then if she was? What if she was?

Solomon knew if he, as *king*, asked her to marry him, she would certainly not deny him. No maiden in the kingdom would. But would she marry him if he were *not* king? This kind of information would be extremely hard to obtain, considering his position. But he realized that, at this moment, he had a unique opportunity to learn this very thing. He had never had a chance like this before, and it was unlikely he ever would again. How does the king hide? Yet, here he was, hidden, and given the rare chance to secure a bride in whom he would never have any doubt. But there was also a risk. What if she chose against him? What then? Could she be compelled to marry him anyway? No, certainly not as queen, at any rate. He sifted the possibilities in his mind.

He did not want to go back to Jerusalem—that was the last thing he wanted. He had been on a journey to Tyre, but there really was no pressing need for him there either. What he needed, what he really needed right now was, well, it was this—a place like this. He needed an escape. A chance to live a simple life in a small, quiet place where he could be alone, away from the pressure, away from the confusion, and alone with his God. Then he remembered his dream of the previous night. The words on the sign stretched out before him, like a clear picture in his mind: "A man's heart prepares his way, but the Lord directs his steps." Quietly, in his own heart and mind, he offered a prayer before the Lord: *God of my fathers, if you have directed me here—if you wish me to do this thing—please speak to me right now.*

The women had been talking softly, but just at that moment, they paused. At precisely that instant, Solomon heard an eagle scream, out past the open door, over the distant hills. The same eagle that had coaxed him out of his tent the night before. The same that caused him to fall down the hill, which led to his being where he was now. The same that hovered over him through the night as he dreamed. Solomon made his decision. He would stay until he had his answer.

Chapter 9

Eventually, Solomon dozed off to sleep. When he awoke, he was alone in the house. He could feel the heat of the sun radiating through the roof of the shanty, warming the room. The women had apparently left him to sleep and had gone off to work for the day. He sat up, carefully placing his injured foot onto the floor. Abishag's headdress was still wrapped around it. Suddenly, he heard a loud snort from just outside the door. His horse! Solomon grabbed his temples.

"Shishak!" he whispered.

His men, of course, would be out looking for him. Unable to track his movements, they must have released his horse to find him. Solomon's favorite horse was a rare Arabian, so white it could almost be considered Albino if not for its fierce black eyes. The overriding characteristic of its unique pedigree was its strong loyalty to one and only one owner. Indeed, the animal had bonded with Solomon when it was a colt and had remained attached ever since. Solomon's men would have known that if released, the horse would find him, and a horse was much easier to track than a man. If his horse was here, it meant he had little time before his guards would arrive as well.

What to do now? Briefly, Solomon considered getting on his mount and fleeing, but quickly dismissed the thought. His guards would still track him. Besides, it was only proper that they know he was safe and well, and soon, before the whole kingdom was called out in search of him. No, he would have to face them. But what then?

Solomon struggled to his feet and hobbled over to the door. A pot of water was there. He splashed some onto his hands and face to freshen his appearance. Underneath the woolen cloak, his clothing was still clean and stately, but he was, of course, missing a boot. There was no time to improvise one; he would have to go meet them as he was and somehow convince them he was healthy and in no need of assistance. He limped out to the horse, which was saddled and bridled. This had surely been a deliberate consideration by his men, surmising that if the horse found Solomon, he might need to ride. They had also packed Shishak with provisions—food and water, bandages, weapons, and money.

With great effort, Solomon swung up onto the mount, wincing in pain as pressure was put on his leg. He draped the woolen cloak in front of him over the horse's shoulders so that it hung down, obscuring his feet on both sides. Then, to a click of Solomon's tongue, the well-trained steed trotted out of the yard and back down the path in the direction from which it had come.

Solomon had not traveled long when he spotted two riders making their way down the side of a not-too-distant ridge, silhouetted against the sky. Their plan to let the horse lead them to him had been a good one. He wheeled his mount over into a tall vineyard that bordered the path and concocted a plan. Then he trotted Shishak back down the path in order to intercept them.

Abishag looked up from where she was harvesting. She was working alone today; her mother had made a trip down to town to get some supplies to care for the stranger. The scream of a soaring eagle echoed through the canyon. That same eagle had been hovering in this area since yesterday. It was odd. Then she noticed the horsemen on the hill. Surprised, she stopped what she was doing and studied them as they worked their way down the ridge. There was no trail there, she knew. Only foxes and shepherds were seen on the upper hills, and the shepherds did not ride horses. What were such men doing out there in mid-day? It was curious.

Then she heard the thumping of hooves on the trail. She looked toward the sound but, being deep into the vineyard, could not see the approaching rider. She heard him pass nearby, however, and the thumping faded off down the hill.

Several fields down, Barkos had also noticed the riders descending the hill, but he was a bit closer to where they would meet the trail. He stopped and watched them, measuring the unknown visitors with a wary eye. Then he also heard the rider on the trail and had a good enough view to identify the unknown companion of Abishag, whom he had encountered early that morning, trotting by.

All day, Barkos had been pondering this stranger who claimed to be Abishag's brother. He did not believe in the least that he was really who he said he was. The fact that Barkos had caught her with a strange man, her veil removed, only confirmed to him what he had believed all along. Like mother, like daughter. The couple's surprise and awkward reaction when he walked up on them proved it. She was a woman of ill repute, an illegitimate daughter of Abelah.

Nonetheless, the man's threat that he had come to claim the land troubled Barkos. It was commonly known that neither of the women really had legal claim to the vineyard that was adjacent to his. Why the wealthy baron, Lord Hamon, permitted the charade to continue, he had no idea. But one thing he did know: It would come to an end. The woman's brothers knew she was not really part of the family. It was only a matter of time until the land was repossessed, and then perhaps, if he finessed the situation successfully, the vineyard would fall to him.

But, Barkos reasoned, the deceitful women certainly knew this, too. They knew the only way they could secure their estate was to somehow "discover" another brother. Perhaps this was what they were attempting now, and if so, it appeared there were others cooperating with their plan.

Barkos, a lonely man far removed from the centers of power, was never given much notice. Baal Hamon, the younger, was poised to inherit a large estate in Shunem when his father passed away, which could be at any time. When that happened, everyone knew there would likely be a shake-up in the status quo.

The heir-apparent was prone to the rewarding of favors, and many were working hard already to win his good will, in order to secure a better place in the coming administration. Barkos realized that this might be an opportunity for him. If he could somehow spoil the women's devious plan and, in the process, present Baal Hamon with a new vineyard, it would go a long way toward securing his own position. Barkos decided he needed to find out what exactly was going on.

He dropped his basket of grapes with a thump, recklessly letting them spill to waste, and then scurried off through the vines in the direction the horseman had headed.

****

"There!" Jachin shouted, pointing down to the trail where Solomon was trotting his mount toward them.

"Thank the Lord!" Boaz exclaimed.

They hurriedly prodded their horses down the steep bank and onto the trail to meet Solomon en route. The king had slowed his horse to a gentle trot, and then a walk, as he neared the place where the men were just now clearing the row of brush that skirted the canyon wall.

"All is well, my friends," he called out to them, holding up his hand in greeting as they hurried to meet him. "All is well."

"My lord, king," Jachin exclaimed, "we are at your service; what do you require?" He dismounted his horse in order to be ready to attend to any need that the king might impart. Solomon stayed on his mount.

"I am a fortunate man," Solomon replied, "whom God has blessed with such wise and loyal guardians as the two of you. Please be assured that I am in need of no special attention, but I do need to speak with you."

They looked him over. He did, in fact, appear to be in perfect vigor.

"We were quite concerned, my lord," Boaz spoke. "We thought perhaps you had been taken, or . . ." He left the sentence unfinished, not wanting to mention that the men had considered him to be suicidal.

Solomon shook his head. "No, no, my friends, not so. If I have been taken by anyone, it was surely the Lord. In his heart a man prepares his steps, but the Lord directs his way. I had intended just to go for a walk, to enjoy one of the glorious sunsets that this valley is known for, but the Lord had other plans. He directed me down here, and I have been in the care of loyal Israelites who live in this valley." He motioned up the trail with a tilt of his head. "I have also learned that there is business for me to attend to here. This is what we must speak about. The Lord spoke to me in a dream last night, and my journey comes to an end in this place, at least for a time."

The men looked at one another. It was a strange turn— Solomon, having "business" in this out-of-the-way place?

"My lord," Jachin asked, "should we break camp and prepare to stay?"

"You will break camp at once," Solomon replied. "But you shall not remain here. What I would have you to understand is, *I* have business in this area; the two of *you* have business elsewhere."

They looked at one another in sudden bewilderment, then back at their king.

"We are sworn not to leave your side, my lord," Jachin whispered, imagining the undesirable lot of a royal guard who returned without his charge.

"Yes, of course," Solomon replied, "and you shall return to my side. But for now, your most excellent services are required elsewhere." He reached into his saddle pouch and produced two rolled documents, each sealed with the royal seal. He handed one to each of the guards.

"Urgent business awaits in Tyre," he explained, "and, Boaz,

you must go there in my stead and deliver this message to Huram-Abi. There is also urgent business in Jerusalem, and, Jachin, you must go there in my stead and deliver this letter to the high priest Zadok. Then you will both return to me here, and I shall give you further instructions."

The two guards stared at him in stunned silence, a more surprising command almost unimaginable.

Meanwhile, Barkos was quickly but carefully working his way through the vines, trying to get close enough to hear the conversation without revealing his presence. He could see the three men passing around what looked like some kind of legal documents. He scurried in closer.

"But, my lord, what about our vows? . . . and you . . ."

"Before whom were your vows made, the Lord or me?"

"Before you, my lord."

"Well, then, I release you from your vows. It is my right to do so. Please be assured that I would not require this of you if it were not of the utmost importance. But please also be assured that I *am* requiring it of you."

The two guards looked at Solomon's face. They had seen this expression before, and the firmness of his tone left no room for doubt. Jachin rubbed his neck and squinted up at the hills in bafflement. Then he looked back at the king.

"As always, my lord, we are at your service, but if I may, what shall we say to those who question us concerning you?"

"You may tell them the Lord has spoken to me, and I am attending to the Lord's business in this place," Solomon answered.

"My lord, we will certainly be asked, so please tell us the nature of . . . the Lord's business."

Solomon pursed his lips. It was a reasonable request. He needed to give a reasonable answer. He stalled before the two loyal guards, in true empathy for their plight, while they patiently waited in concerned confusion.

122

"Brothers, if you must know, I have kinsmen here, kinsmen you do not know. The fact of the matter is, the ownership of these vineyards is in doubt, and I need to remain for a time to set to right that which is wrong. Israelites are oppressed, and the Lord has ordained me to liberate them. I dare not shirk this duty. Yet the messages I gave you must be delivered. I will stay and finalize the repatriation of the land. After the property is secure, we will reunite here."

Barkos's eyes grew wide as he listened, catching some of the dialog, but not all. So it *was* a plot to steal the land! And well organized, too. The man and the two riders appeared to be finely dressed and well financed. This was a situation to be taken seriously. He leaned forward. At that moment, a dry twig snapped loudly under his foot. The three men turned quickly, the guards reaching for their swords. Barkos sank down low into the vines and remained very still.

The trio searched the vines with their eyes. But perceiving nothing, after a few moments, they relaxed.

"It is just a fox; they are a plague around here," Solomon said. "This is a peaceful little place; you need not worry about me. Come, let us ride on as we converse. I am actually traveling to town."

The guards remounted, and the three men moved down the path a bit.

When they had disappeared over the hill, Barkos scurried out of his hideout and rushed back to his own vineyard, his heart thumping wildly. His mind was racing. He would have to inform Baal Hamon.

****

Solomon and his two men continued to converse as they rode side by side.

"My lord, are you in need of any provisions before we . . . part ways? Should we not return to camp and leave you well prepared?" Jachin asked.

"Truly I thrive under the blessing of your care," Solomon

replied, "but as I said, I have kinsmen here; they can supply me. I have plenty of gold, as you know, and the business I have to attend to is urgent, as is yours."

The throbbing in Solomon's ankle reminded him that he did, in fact, have urgent business—the care of his foot. The bone would need to be set soon, he knew. And he did not want to spend too much time with the men, lest they discover his injury. If they were to learn of it, they would certainly prefer death than to leave his side. As they came to the place where the guards would leave the trail and head back up the hill toward camp, Solomon turned his horse around and faced them. They looked back at him with loyal attention.

"My friends," he said, "here we part ways, for a time. If you carry out the mission I have given you with the same honor and diligence as you have displayed while by my side, I will be most grateful. Do not find yourselves faltering or fearful, and if you encounter hardship, remember that I am depending on you. The messages you carry are important, and the seal on those letters is to be broken only by those to whom they are addressed. When we meet again, you will be rewarded for this unusual service. May the Lord be with you."

The two guards, with great reluctance and uttering desperate urges for the king to be wary, bade farewell to their master. Vowing to return, they turned to embark on the most terrifying mission their loyal hearts could imagine: leaving their charge.

The unlikely parting successfully accomplished, Solomon continued down the path toward Shunem. For the first time he could remember, he was truly alone, unknown, and in a strange place.

Alone did not fully account for the sensation that crept over him. He was now fully responsible for his own protection, a situation which he could scarcely remember facing in his life. The defense of a king was an art which Jachin and Boaz had brought to new levels of perfection. Boaz, the appointed commander in the event of an attack on the king, was an expert in the throwing arts, while Jachin specialized in attack with the sword. Boaz, ambidextrous and loaded with knives and throwing axes, had so honed his skills that he could have several projectiles in the air simultaneously, pulling and swinging with both right and left hand in rapid succession. If the assailants were dressed in armor, the axes were thrown. Even if the weapons didn't pierce the armor, they would most certainly down the attacker so that Jachin could finish him off with the sword.

In the event of a quick attack, Boaz's knives would be in the attacker's chest almost before he knew they were coming, having turned perfect revolutions in the air to land blade into flesh. His art required tremendous concentration, and nerves as steely as his blades, for the throws and revolutions were practiced at exact distances. A knife thrown too soon would hit harmlessly, blunt end on the target. To be effective, it was imperative that Boaz remain in a fixed position, which served well his job of keeping the king behind him, while he assessed the attack and called out orders to Jachin. Jachin's skill and brute strength with a sword gave him the ability to charge and subdue or detain attackers long enough for Boaz's well-placed projectiles to find their targets.

In practice sessions, Jachin was accustomed to hearing dummy knives whiz past his ears as Boaz barked out orders: "Left! . . . Right! . . . Down!" Were real knives in the air, he would have to lurch instantly . . . or die.

For longer throws, Boaz was also counted among the mighty men of David who practiced with sling and stone, the champion of those who could target a stone to a hair's breadth and not miss. Solomon also carried knives and could re-arm Boaz, or even throw knives in his own defense if the situation became sufficiently desperate. He did not, however, throw as well as Boaz.

If this method of defense were executed to perfection, it was unlikely that any but the most overwhelming attack could reach the king, for attacking ranks would already be thinned by guards farther out along the fringe. So well trained was the king's entourage that war games showed that to have any hope of victory, an attacking enemy must outnumber the defense by a minimum of three to one. This bit of information was a fine deterrent; fighting men, not being fools, would not be anxious to try their odds at being the one out of three who survived.

The reputation of the defense was deliberately published widely, while its secrets were withheld, a strategy designed to make the recruiting of would-be assassins difficult. No attacker would survive to explain their defeat, and any new attacker would have no intelligence upon which to devise an improved assault. Among future generations, the defense would be known as "Solomon's Shield," for it was Solomon who had designed it, and in military games, it had proven stunningly effective.

Now, for the first time Solomon could remember, he was without this protection. It felt surreal to be so far from Jerusalem, far from his constant responsibilities, far, even, from anyone who would recognize him—to be alone—all alone, not knowing what would happen next, or even truly why he was here. All of Solomon's life had been carefully scripted for him, until this moment. If there was a God in heaven who ordered the steps of man, there was plenty of room for Him to do it now.

Chapter 10

Baal Hamon. It was a name that had been infamous in the town of Shunem for over forty years. Even the town and the territory surrounding it was often referred to as "Baal Hamon country." Baal Hamon, the elder, had earned this prominence through his cleverly acquired wealth and his political skill in keeping it. He was, however, fading into the background as age and sickness diminished his influence, while his eldest son gradually assumed control of the affairs of his father's sprawling estate. Tall, good-looking, and cunning, this son was already observed to have inherited a dangerous share of his father's political acumen, but was yet unseasoned with the gentleness of age. His rising profile excited well-founded nervousness in the local population.

Baal Hamon, the younger, sat in a meeting with his advisors following his mid-day meal. The heat of the sun at its zenith added to his already barely contained desire to nap rather than work. The meeting was really just a formality; he was well acquainted with the affairs of his estate, his quick mind absorbing and recalling details effortlessly. But his counselors had been loyal to his father, and the time with the fortune's heir meant more to them than to himself. Hamon needed to afford them the courtesy of his attention just to keep the wheels of goodwill turning smoothly. He would have preferred to spend the time with his peers, who, in fact, were his informal advisors. Their opinions,

127

given in his kitchen or in the drinking rooms or while out hunting, ultimately carried more weight in his policy decisions than the ramblings of his father's aged friends. However, these men were respected in the community, and Hamon was savvy enough to know that he could not succeed without them. Their voices were needed to advertise his plans in a favorable light to the community and the local judges.

Ono, who had been the estate's accountant for longer than anyone could remember, was just beginning his weekly report, reviewing for Hamon in excruciating detail the state of his various accounts, of who owed what and how much and by when. Hamon's father had insisted upon this detail, but to Hamon, who was fresh off a particularly large and satisfying lunch, Ono's droning voice was an insomniac's miracle cure.

Hamon pushed his chair back and rose from his seat, wandering over to the window to peek out through the lattice as the aged accountant droned on. Hamon's tower was the highest building in town. Its upper windows provided a luscious view of the entire city and the fields surrounding it. Hamon squinted out, noticing a figure moving down the street toward his building at a bustling pace quite out of place in the mid-afternoon calm. His awkward limp identified him instantly: Barkos. Was he coming here? Hamon hoped so.

Barkos, a distant relative, was normally not afforded much of the baron's attention, but under the circumstances, Hamon would accept any excuse to be relieved of the present monotony. He sauntered back to his seat and waited hopefully for an interruption. Eventually, there was indeed a knock on the door, and a young woman poked her head in.

"Excuse me, lords?"

Ono stopped briefly and looked up from his notes.

"Sylva, what is it?" Hamon asked.

"I am sorry to disturb you, my lord, but there is someone here to see you—he insists it is quite important."

"That's quite all right, Sylva. My brother, Caleh, will hear the rest of this report," Hamon said, slapping his hand on the shoulder of his younger brother as he passed by toward the door. Caleb gave him a thankless glance. If Hamon was bored by these meetings, his brother was even more so, but with sadistic delight, Hamon insisted he attend them all.

Hamon glided down the hallway in no particular hurry, following his half-sister, Sylva. If all went well, he might be able to miss the entire meeting. He turned off into a side room.

"Send him to me here," he called out as he entered.

Shortly, Barkos scuffled into the room. Hamon noticed that his visitor was sweaty and disheveled from his hurried trip into town. It would be the second trip for Barkos that day, having already been down for the morning market. Hamon knew he would not go to the trouble for no reason. Nonetheless, Barkos had always, for him, been easy to tease.

"Forget your basket again, Barkos?"

Barkos appraised Hamon's casual manner. He appeared to be doing nothing at all and to be in no particular hurry. Under normal circumstances, he might have been offended by Hamon's unabashed jabs, but this time, he was just glad to get an audience with him, and it appeared he had Hamon's full attention. Perhaps this would go well.

"My lord," Barkos began, "I have news—very important news—to report."

Hamon observed Barkos's grave tone and expression with amusement. He was sure the news was important to Barkos, but doubted it would be as important to himself.

"Very important news, hmm?" Hamon answered, leaning back and stroking his chin. "I was just hearing very important news. In fact, I was interrupted from a meeting in which the finances of my estate were being discussed. Is your very important news equal to that?"

"My lord," Barkos continued, leaning forward and maintaining the grave tone and expression, "as you know, my vineyard is up on the northwest hill, adjacent to the one farmed by the widow, Abelah, and her daughter. Of course, you realize that it is a very choice piece of land these women farm, producing much fruit."

Hamon was amused by the man. He knew that Barkos wanted to improve his position, as did many others in this town, but his attempts to attract Hamon's attention by referencing things he thought would interest him were transparent and quaint.

"I am aware that it's a fine vineyard, a very fine vineyard," Hamon replied. "Am I to be impressed with repetitions of things which I already know?"

"Yes, I . . . I mean, no, but, well, what I-I mean is . . ."

Hamon let his eyes roll back and feigned a snore.

"What I mean is, I know you have been acquiring land in that area, and I have learned that this particular vineyard may be going through a change in ownership soon—*very* soon!" he blurted.

Now he had Hamon's attention in truth, but Hamon was well practiced at concealing his thoughts.

"Go on."

"It is true that you have not been able to acquire this vineyard from those women, is it not?"

On this point Barkos was incorrect. It was, in fact, well within Hamon's power to obtain that particular vineyard, but his reason for not doing so was a mystery he enjoyed keeping to himself. Doing so allowed Barkos's and others' imaginations to speculate on unlikely things, such as the theory Barkos had just espoused.

In fact, his reasons for not acquiring the land were more personal than political, for Hamon had known Abishag since she was a child growing up. He had observed her in the early days of womanhood, before she had taken to wearing the virgin's veil, and he knew of her beauty. He also knew that her absence from the area had been because, as the loveliest maiden in all the land, she was selected to serve King David in his old age. The rumor had spread throughout the valley that Abishag had actually run off with a Phoenician trader, but Hamon knew the truth. He knew it from Abishag's own lips, and he had confirmed it through his sources in Jerusalem.

Her service in the royal courts had made her a fascinating person, even more so than before. She was someone to be sided with, not against, considering the contacts she might still have in Jerusalem. The fact was, Hamon did not take her land because he was planning to marry her—at the right time.

He had little doubt that she would agree to his proposal. She had many problems that such an arrangement would instantly solve. She was plagued by a poor reputation; becoming the wife of the richest man in town would certainly remedy that. She was poor and had a widowed mother to care for; everyone knew that would not be a problem if she were in Hamon's care. And she had to slave in the fields every day to survive, working much harder than a girl probably wanted to. As Hamon's wife, she would be respected, wealthy, and have servants of her own. She had every reason to accept his proposal. But he allowed the situation to linger as it was, priming her to jump at the chance when he came to rescue her.

For now, Hamon played along with Barkos's assumption.

"It would be a fine vineyard to obtain. Why do you say the ownership is in doubt?"

"As you know, Baal Hamon, the ownership has always been in doubt, but now I may be able to prove it. The women have conspired to have a man show up who claims to be the maiden's brother and to make a claim on the land!" he gushed.

Hamon regarded the nervous little man warily. Was this the product of a paranoid imagination, or was Barkos really onto something?

"And you know this because. . .?" Hamon asked, leaning forward.

Barkos, too, leaned forward, and his voice dropped lower.

"I met him. I saw him in the vineyard. He told me so himself. He claimed to be her brother. And later, I overheard him speaking on the trail, discussing the matter with two very well-dressed men on fine horses. It is a conspiracy, of course, for we know all her brothers."

"Yes . . . yes, of course," Hamon agreed. But he knew a bit more about Abishag's family than most people did. His father had briefed him on all the local families and their backgrounds, with detailed knowledge that had been forgotten by many of the current generation. Though rumor had it that Abishag was illegitimate, Hamon knew it was not true. He also knew that it was likely Abishag did, in fact, have a missing brother, one who one day might return to claim land. Hamon's father had warned him about this possibility. It was another reason Abishag would be useful as a wife, for if he acquired the land through marriage, it would be more secure against such a raid.

"And here is the other part," Barkos continued, pausing baitingly.

"Yes?"

"I saw them . . . *together*."

"Together? What do you mean?" Hamon asked.

"She had her veil off. It was early morning and she had her veil off, and they were embracing on the trail. It's her Phoenician lover!"

Hamon stared at Barkos with barely hidden skepticism. He knew that Abishag's character would never stoop to such a thing, no matter what others thought.

"What do you mean, *embracing*?"

"They were like this," Barkos whispered, reaching his arm out to the side in imitation of holding an imaginary person around the shoulders. "Eh?" Barkos nudged, his eyebrows shooting up.

Hamon did not consider what Barkos was describing to be a lovers' embrace at all. But for Abishag to be seen with her veil off was indeed unusual. If true, it could only mean one thing: The man was, in fact, her brother, returning, just as Barkos had said, to claim the land. Hamon knew that Abishag would never behave with a stranger so casually.

"If what you have said is true, this is most interesting, most interesting indeed," Hamon replied, staring up at the ceiling in thought.

Barkos leaned back, pleased with himself.

"I thought you would want to know. And, of course, if justice is done in this matter, and the vineyard does return to us as rightful owners, you know that it could easily be combined with mine," Barkos hinted.

Hamon was amused at the man's use of the word "us." With Hamon, everyone wanted to be "us." He knew that Barkos's status as a distant relative excited in him more hope than Hamon would ever justify with favors. But no, Barkos would never have any more land than he already possessed, and would be lucky to keep that. Nonetheless, the information he provided was worthy of attention and serious thought.

"Barkos, you have been very helpful. I think you deserve a drink." Hamon reached into his pouch and pulled out a couple of copper pieces. "Here, go enjoy yourself."

Barkos smiled. The meeting had gone better than he could have imagined.

"Thank you," he replied with an excited grin. He took the coins and rose to leave.

"Oh, and one more thing, Barkos," Hamon said, causing the visitor to freeze and look back at him. "Tell no one of this matter until we decide what to do, all right?"

"Of course!" he replied. He left the room and went bouncing down the street, merrily tossing the coins up in the air and catching them as he went.

But Hamon sat where he was for a long time, his clever mind probing all the possible ramifications of this unexpected turn of events.

Chapter 11

The glory of young men is their strength: and the beauty of old men is the gray head.

—Proverbs 20:29

As Solomon guided his steed down the trail toward town, he became aware of a greater concentration of houses, huts, and different kinds of buildings. Abishag's residence was at the very edge of plantable land. As Solomon descended into flatter terrain, wheat and barley replaced the grapevines, and he noticed workers out in the fields tending the crops. If he could see them, they could see him. He became conscious of his appearance, and that of his brilliant horse, which would certainly attract the attention of passersby on the trail. It was suddenly urgent that he find a way to blend in, but he needed his mount badly. He could not travel without it. He pulled up near a grove of trees and considered what to do, looking all around him.

Then Solomon noticed a small brook watering the grove. His eyes followed its path up through a draw in the hills. If there was a brook, there would surely be livestock nearby. He broke from the trail and followed the brook up the draw. After passing through a narrow, the draw widened into a hidden canyon. He found himself on a sheep trail that wound its way up the canyon alongside the brook. Upon rounding a bend, a farmyard became visible at the end of a long field. Sheep and goats grazed in the canyon. A livestock farm. Solomon nudged his horse forward, trotting him out across the field toward the house and barn.

Shammai, the aged livery farmer, looked up from the hide he was tanning to see a strange rider approaching from across the fields. He squinted at him, wiping the sweat from his forehead with the back of his hand. What was this? He dropped the hide back into the tanning brine and rinsed off his hands in a bucket of water. It was not every day that a visitor was found all the way up here, and an unusual-looking visitor at that.

Shammai walked out toward the approaching rider and stopped to lean on a wooden rail fence surrounding a stone water trough. As the visitor drew closer, Shammai saw that the horse was truly splendid and that the rider sat him like a king. The mounting equipment was of excellent quality also.

"Shalom!" Solomon called out as he approached the old farmer.

"Shalom," the man replied, looking curiously up at the stranger, and then down at his magnificent steed. "I am Shammai, of Issachar. Whom do you seek, my lord?"

"I am called Jedidiah," he replied. "I have traveled far, and am in search of care and boarding for my horse. Do you know where I might find a stable?"

The farmer studied the rider's face.

"Care for your horse, you say?" he said, allowing himself a long look at the mount. "My lord, I have been caring for livestock for forty years, and I do not believe I have ever seen a stallion to equal yours. No doubt it is used to much better care that can be provided here, but we do have some basic things. There is not much care for livestock here in Baal Hamon country, but the best you will find is right here in my stable. Where are you traveling, if I may ask? And how long do you wish to stay?"

"I would like to rest my horse, my lord, for the night at least, but I also must visit town before sundown. If you would permit me to borrow a donkey, I would be willing to leave my horse with you as security," Solomon said.

The man chuckled in disbelief. He looked back at the horse, standing majestically with its deep chest, clear eyes, and perfect behavior. It showed no sign of needing a rest.

"Your horse, as security for my donkey?" he asked. "And just how will I be assured that you will not disappear with my donkey, and leave me stuck with this horse of yours? Your offer leaves me with too little risk, my lord, and that I find risky."

Solomon smiled at the man, discerning the sense in his objection. An elderly Israelite deserved a certain amount of forthrightness. Though their conversation had been short, Solomon had already decided that he could trust the man.

"My lord, you are Shammai of Issachar, as you say, an Israelite of distinguished birth. I am Jedidiah of Judah, and am en route to Jerusalem, on the business of your king. But I travel alone. I carry gold, my lord, and am not known in this land. I fear if I ride a stallion such as this into a poor village, I may as well wear my gold on my sleeve, for I will surely attract the attention of the trail raider. Besides which, I have another problem."

With that, Solomon pulled up the cloak that was hanging down, to reveal his bootless foot. The man peered at his wrapped ankle.

"My lord, my ankle is broken, I do fear," he said, "and I am in search of a physician. I am in no position to defend myself, should the need arise. If you would be so kind as to care for my horse and loan me a donkey, I will certainly pay you fairly," Solomon said.

"That is an answer I can believe," the man responded, breaking away from the rail and heading toward the barn. "Come this way, and I'll provide what you need."

Solomon found Shammai of Issachar to be exceedingly helpful, once his trust had been won. A noble man, worthy of his noble name. He fixed Solomon up with a young, steady mount.

The man's wife, a lovely little woman by the name of Ruth, came out then and refreshed him with cold water and a satchel of food to take on his way. Then Shammai helped Solomon mount up again and gave him clear directions on just how to locate the one and only physician who practiced in Shunem, a man by the name of Jockshan. As Solomon was turning to ride out, the man stuck a long thick shepherd's cane into his hand.

"You may find this helpful," he grinned, "that is, if you have any intention to dismount when you arrive."

Solomon laughed, thanked the kindly old man and his wife, and headed back toward town in search of Jockshan, the physician. With his woolen cloak wrapped around him, his simple turban on his head, and the shepherd's cane in his hand, he attracted no attention at all as he traveled down the path on his newly acquired donkey.

It was now mid-afternoon, and as the trail neared the city proper, it became increasingly crowded with laborers, women carrying water, and domestic animals.

Shunem had no city wall, being just a little hamlet in the hills, but in the custom of many small towns, it boasted a stone arch in lieu of a gate at its entrance. Without this, it would be difficult to discern the entrance, for the town blended into the countryside around it.

Next to the gate, on the inside, stone benches were situated, where the leaders of the city met to judge cases. On a day like today, the benches were used as hitching posts, places to set bundles while loading pack animals, and for various other, less distinguished uses. Nonetheless, there were a few graybeards lounging there, happy to spend the day watching the simple commerce that passed by. Being locals, they knew well all who passed on a normal day and noted curiously the unknown shepherd on the donkey.

Solomon found the main street of Shunem to be typical of those in dozens of villages in rural Israel. It led to a central square which featured a vegetable market and a few shops with various other kinds of wares. Nothing too exotic. A leather shop, a metal smith, and shops of miscellaneous handmade goods: sandals, clothing, baskets . . . according to the talents of the local population. Nothing imported was displayed. The only thing that distinguished Shunem from many other Israelite towns of its size was its disproportionate number of drinking rooms, owing, no doubt, to the easy availability of grapes for the making of wine.

Solomon blended into the mid-afternoon crowd, following the landmarks given him, toward a stone building off the main market area, where Jockshan the physician made his practice.

****

Back at their home, Abishag and her mother were concerned about their missing guest. They found the horse tracks leading up to the house and away, and they knew that their visitor had no horse. They also realized he had left without taking any provisions from the house that they could tell. They knew that he did not have any supplies with him and that he was injured. Was he a man on the run, and had his pursuers caught up with him? He did not strike Abishag as that kind of a man. If he was kidnapped, she tended to believe he must be the innocent party, chased by evildoers, but she could not explain why. He seemed . . . well, he just seemed above that. But why would an injured man leave a comfortable house, taking no provisions with him, of his own free will? It did not make sense. As the day stretched toward evening, their puzzlement drifted toward worry.

Finally, with little light left in the day, Abishag declared, "I'm going down to town."

"But it's getting late, dear."

"I realize that. That is why I should be going now, if I am to be going at all."

"And what will you do when you get there?" Abelah asked.

"I don't exactly know. Perhaps I will inquire at the gate; see if anyone has seen him. A man with a broken ankle would be memorable if seen, don't you think? He may be my brother, after all. Must I not try?"

Her mother glanced out apprehensively at the diminishing day.

"Be careful, please."

****

As Solomon neared his destination, the crowd thinned a bit, and he came upon a row of beggars gathered against a stone wall. Many of them were children, dressed in tattered rags, peering up at him out of dark hoods. Also in this area were the infirm, lame, crippled, blind, and those generally unfit to work. There was not a great number of them, but the sight troubled him nonetheless. Such open misery was not seen in Jerusalem, particularly nowadays when wealth was abundant. His own hospital had cleared the streets of most of the infirm, and children were always cared for in Jerusalem. He moved on, leaving the compassion that welled in him unfulfilled for the moment.

As Solomon drew closer to the building of the physician, he observed that it was, in fact, a busy place. Oddly, smoke ascended from its chimneystack, though it was not cold. Benches were situated outside the door, and a peculiar collection of humanity sat along them. He rode up and ducked down to glance through the open door, discovering that the small waiting room inside was also full.

"Excuse me, lord," called a woman from a nearby bench. "I don't think they will let you ride your donkey in there, and even if they did, I have been waiting here since this morning and . . ." Suddenly, she let loose with a horrific-sounding cough and continued to hack for several moments. Solomon recognized the disease instantly. It was a lung infection, commonly contracted from those who traveled in Africa. He had studied it and written about it, and treatment in Jerusalem had all but wiped out the disease there. It thrived in humid climates, which made it odd to see such an advanced case on the outskirts of Jezreel in the summer.

"You have the African swamp fever," he declared, almost out of habit.

"That's not what Jockshan calls it," she croaked, "but anyway, as I was saying, there are a lot of us in line here, and you'd better be prepared to . . ." Again, she launched into a fit of coughing.

Solomon looked around at the folks waiting and soon realized the majority of those present had the same infirmity. The swamp fever was hard to treat, not because the germ was hard to kill, but because the treatment required was opposite of that which supplied the patient relief. The more humid the climate, the more relief came to the patient's lungs, but also, the greater the progress of the disease. While most infections of this type were treated with moist air, this one was unusual in that it required dry. The germ could be killed if the patient were fed a healthy diet and made to breathe hot, dry air, as in a kiln. A swallow of an oil-based ointment several times a day could moisten the throat enough to provide relief from the pain until the germ perished.

A man sauntered out of the building, perspiring, his face flushed red as though he had come out of a hot bath. He appeared very relaxed and wandered away with a dreamy expression on his face as though he had just been relieved of great suffering. Solomon caught a whiff of mint spices on his clothing as he drifted by and disappeared around a corner.

"All right, who is next?" a young, sincere-looking man called from inside the doorway.

A chorus of voices responded, but in the end, one person was singled out, and the room calmed down again.

"Excuse me, daughter," Solomon said to the woman who had spoken to him. "What kind of treatment are they giving you in there?"

"Steam bath," she croaked. "Jockshan has a special herb bath that is the only thing that works on this ailment."

"Steam bath!"

She looked at him strangely. "Yes, that's right, steam bath. And don't think you're getting in there ahead of me!"

He eyed her expertly. This was not turning out to be a very fruitful trip. One doctor in town, and he could not get in to see him. Even if he could, from what he was hearing, he did not know if he wanted to. He looked around at the waiting crowd. This appeared to be a one-ailment clinic. If anyone were to come with another kind of problem, such as he just had, there was little chance they could even get in. He looked back down at the woman.

"Tell me, dear woman, just how long have you had this ailment?"

"One and one-half years," she answered. "Jockshan says it's getting better and that I just have to be patient and let the treatment work, but I'm running out of money to pay for it."

Her disease was reaching a critical stage. Solomon knew, that by now, a large portion of her lungs was in danger of being permanently destroyed. If she did not stop the progress of the disease soon, she would be beyond recovery.

"Looks like you have an epidemic here," he said, motioning to the people around him.

"Yes, and it looks like you are not from around here," she answered. "Listen, I do not want to be rude, but it's been a week since my last treatment and it's really painful to talk right now, so if you don't mind . . ." She began coughing again.

Solomon shook his head in disgusted amazement. What kind of doctor would continue to prescribe the same treatment year after year, when it was obvious it was not working? He swung his donkey around and headed back toward the market. If his leg was going to be set, it looked like he would have to do it himself.

He worked his way back toward the main street, looking for a shop that could provide him with the necessary supplies. He passed a bakery, and the smell of fresh bread wafted out toward him as a wave of heat from the fire oven hit his face. Farther on, he found a basket shop, next to a lamp dealer.

Solomon took his staff and leaned off the donkey, putting his weight on it. Then he swung his injured leg around behind the animal, and slid down the rod, landing on his good foot. He wrapped the reins to a post and hobbled into the basket shop. A plump little woman was working there.

"What can I help you find?" she asked.

"Well, I don't need a basket, but I need some basket supplies, if you are willing to sell them. Do you have bamboo rods?"

"Going to make your own basket, eh?"

"No, I need them for something else." He knew the rods could be placed around his ankle and then bound together with a cloth to keep the bones straight, once he had them set in place.

"Well, I don't have bamboo rods, but how about these dried vine stalks?" she asked, holding up some thick, dark brown stalks.

Solomon tested them in his hands. They would serve his purpose, though unconventional. He paid the woman and hobbled back out of the shop to continue on his donkey.

Glancing down at the lamp seller's table, he noticed some flasks of various oils. He dismounted to smell them, then selected one and bought it, flask and all, along with several pinches of selected spices from another nearby merchant. He sprinkled the spices into the flask and shook it up, letting them soak into the oil in a thick mixture. Then, with some effort, he hoisted himself onto the donkey again and headed back down the street.

Stopping by the bakery, Solomon called through the door. A fat little man poked his head out. "What do you want?"

"I apologize, my lord," Solomon explained, "but my leg is injured, and it pains me much to mount and dismount this donkey."

"I see," the man said. "Well, what can I do for you?"

"A loaf of fresh bread, if you don't mind," Solomon said.

The man disappeared for a moment, then came back with a wrapped bundle.

"That will be two Gerahs."

Solomon reached into his pouch. He didn't have much small change. He had just used up all the small pieces with his last two purchases. The smallest he had was a one-Minah gold piece, but Israelite commerce trafficked in silver only. Solomon did some quick math. His smallest gold member was worth twenty-five-hundred times the man's price for the bread. He pulled out the gold piece and held it low where the man could see it. The little baker's eyes widened.

"I don't suppose you have change, do you?" Solomon asked.

"Friend, I would have to sell bread for a year before I'd see a Minah's worth of gold!" the man answered. "No, I do not have change for that!"

"Well, in that case, perhaps we can agree on an arrangement," Solomon said. "Would you benefit from some hired help?"

"Excuse me?"

"My lord, I need your fine bread, but I have no change with which to buy it, so if I give you this gold piece, you owe me something in return, do you not?" Solomon asked.

"Yes, that goes without saying, but I already told you, I don't have any ch—"

"What I am suggesting is that you pay me back by hiring someone I know who needs a job. You can use the change to pay them. Tell me, who keeps your fire room hot?"

"I do," he replied. "I do all the work here myself."

"Well, then," Solomon replied, "May I suggest that you let someone else tend your fire for a couple of weeks. A hard-working man like yourself would appreciate a lighter work load for a time, would you not?"

"You got that right!" he replied. "Look, I don't know why you want that loaf of bread so bad, but if it makes you happy, I'll play along. Send your man over."

"It's a woman." Solomon replied. "And you must do one other thing for me. Do not let her in the front of the store, where the bread is; just employ her out back, in the fire room. She can keep the fire hot for you. Can you promise me that?"

"Sure, whatever you say, friend," the man replied with a pleased but bewildered look on his face.

Solomon explained how much to pay the woman for her

service, which would leave the man with plenty left over, in case Solomon decided to use his services again. As he was riding away, the man motioned quickly to a neighboring merchant and began talking to him excitedly about what had just happened.

Solomon rounded the corner and came upon the street that was home to Jockshan the physician's healing room. Sun had lowered to a shallow angle, causing the streets between buildings to be in full shadow. Soon the air would be cooling. He approached the woman he had been speaking to before. She was still waiting in line, her head bowed down into her clothing, a hoarse sound emanating from her lungs as she breathed.

"Excuse me, dear woman," Solomon said.

She looked up at him.

"You again?"

"Yes, daughter. I have been thinking about your problem, and I found a way for you to get some money for your treatment."

She stared at him uncertainly.

"Would you step over this way for just a moment?" he asked, wanting to get her away from the listening crowd.

"Oh, very well," she resigned herself with an irritated shrug. "I'm not going in for a while anyway."

She dropped her travel satchel by the wall to save her place in line. When they had moved a few paces away from the crowd, Solomon asked her, "How many treatments would twelve silver shekels buy you?"

She laughed, and then coughed.

"That would get me about three months' worth, but where am I going to get twelve silver shekels?"

"I will tell you," he said, "but first may I ask you to do one thing for me?"

"And what is that?"

He pulled out the flask of mixture. "Kindly take two swallows of this. Not all at once, but hold it in your mouth for a moment,

145

and then two swallows, very slowly."

She eyed him warily. "What is it?"

"It's a natural remedy—oil-based, with a bit of spice mixed in, this and that. Here, smell it."

The woman leaned forward and sniffed.

"Hmm," she said, recognizing the smells as fairly common. Then she looked up at him, still skeptical.

Solomon reached into his pouch and pulled out another gold piece, casually flipping it in his thumb and forefinger.

Her eyes followed its movements until she grabbed the flask with some violence and tipped it up, taking it down just as he had directed. The ointment seeped down her throat like warm honey, giving her instant relief. She looked back up at him with wonder.

"Who are you?"

"I am King Solomon."

She smirked. "Right—and I am the Queen of Sheba. You tempt me with relief and then tease me with nonsense. Who are you, really?—some kind of doctor? Where did you get this medicine?"

"I suppose I am a doctor of sorts, but my name—that is more complicated."

She eyed him suspiciously. "Ah. Hiding from the law, eh? Very well, then, I won't ask you any more questions, but could you at least give me the recipe for your potion?"

"The recipe? No, I am afraid that is a secret, but I can offer you something better: a way for you to obtain the money you need. Do you know the baker?"

"Bornio? Yes, of course I know the baker."

"I have spoken to him in your behalf. He is going to hire you to tend his fire for a few weeks. Your pay will be twelve shekels."

She stared at him in disbelief, frozen in place as if in a trance.

"Do you want me to take you over there, too?"

"No, no," she replied, "but . . . but . . . what do I tell him?"

"Just tell him you were sent to tend his fire. Trust me, he will know what to do. He is waiting for you."

"All right, my lord," she replied with a bit more respect, "and thank you, my lord!"

"And one more thing," Solomon said. "Kindly take this flask of medicine, too."

"By all means!" she replied, holding her hand to her chest where the soothing ointment was, even now, warm inside her. She reached out with her other hand to take the flask, but Solomon pulled it back.

"But you must do one more thing. Promise me."

"I promise!" she blurted, realizing afterward that she had no idea what he was going to ask.

"You must stay out of Jockshan's healing room for that full time."

She blinked at him. "Bu- . . . but . . ."

"Four weeks!" Solomon commanded with all the presence of the king he was, resounding in his voice.

"Yes, yes, my lord!" she reacted instinctively, surprising herself that she submitted to his command so quickly. The man had a certain air about him, one that seemed to inspire obedience, even when one didn't know him. "I mean, thank you, my lord!" she added quickly.

"That's better now. After you have done as I said, I will return and give you more of this medicine."

Solomon turned and spurred his donkey down the street and around the corner, leaving her to stare at him in wonder.

****

The sky was now darkening. As Solomon proceeded back toward the market, he realized that the city was transforming around him. Some of the merchants were closing up shop, and others were already gone. The crowd was thinning of children and women, while working folks, who had little interest in shopping, were making their way directly toward their destinations for the evening. Solomon caught a whiff of the cold air he had experienced the night before, and now discerned its source. Down below the city were the swamps, and up from them an occasional a gust of cool, moist air braced his skin.

As some shops closed, others opened, and torches were lit, and flickered over some doorways. Solomon was hungry. He wondered what Abishag and her mother's reaction would be when they came home and found him gone. He would return, but his absence would require an explanation. They would want to know where he had gone, and why. And where did he get this donkey on which he would come riding?

His stomach growled. He set his attention toward finding something to eat before returning to the vineyard farm. Then he remembered the package of trail foods that the kindly farmer's wife had sent with him. He searched inside his clothing for it as he moved back up toward the center of town.

Just then, a beggar scurried up to him with his hand out, limping awkwardly on a lame leg.

"Mercies for the poor?" he asked, his eyes looking up earnestly.

Solomon looked around. Other beggars were crouched at the wall, watching carefully. No doubt they recognized him as a stranger, and wanted to find out if he was favorable toward their needs. Solomon pulled out a couple of ripe figs.

"Tell me," he asked the man, "how did you get into this condition?"

The beggar eyed the figs. He would prefer money, but food was never to be refused.

"I must tell you in order to get those?" he asked.

Solomon handed the figs to him.

"No, you need tell me only because I asked." Solomon recognized that he was truly a beggar. A drunkard would have held out for money, not figs.

"You see the condition of my leg," the man replied, taking a mouthful of the juicy fig. "Labor is very difficult for me. I am unproductive, and no one wants to hire me."

"So you are not an Israelite, then?" Solomon asked, knowing that an Israelite would have a family with inheritance land.

"An Israelite—why, yes, I am an Israelite from Issachar."

"And where is your family's estate?" Solomon asked. "Certainly you could work there?"

"Hmmph," the man replied, eyeing the stranger curiously. "You must just be passing through this area."

Then the beggar noticed the shepherd's staff in Solomon's hand and was struck with perhaps the true intent of his questioning. "Would you hire me, my lord?" he asked. "I cannot walk very well, but given a donkey to ride, I could tend flocks."

Solomon observed the man's eager desperate expression, and pitied him.

"Brother, if I had flocks here, perhaps that could be arranged," he replied, "but if you were reconciled to your family, you would not need to work for a stranger. What stands in the way of that?"

The man shook his head.

"I am not in conflict with my family. My brothers have moved out of this area to make lives for themselves elsewhere. I alone remain here so that perhaps one day . . ." His voice trailed off as he stared out into space, munching on the second of the figs.

The other beggars were watching the exchange carefully.

Solomon was curious about the rest of the story. His years on the judgment seat had cast his mind into the habit of seeking out the answers to situations as he encountered them. Instinctively, he believed that if he knew the circumstances, he could help the man.

"What is your name, if you don't mind?" Solomon asked kindly, rousing the man from his thought.

"My name?" he asked, as if it were a question he was not often asked. "My name is Jared."

"Well, Jared," Solomon said, "you are an Israelite, as am I. That makes us brothers, even if your tribal brothers have moved away, as you say. If you tell me the rest of your story, perhaps I can be of some assistance. But even if not, what have you lost?"

The man nodded. "I can see, my lord, that you are not from this place, and if you wish to stay here with your flocks for any measure of time, there are things you should know."

Solomon observed the man expertly. The longer he talked with him, the less he seemed like a beggar. More like a worthy man, perhaps even an educated man; someone who had been displaced by some strange circumstance that he did not want to tell.

"I want to hear the story, whether I stay or not," Solomon said loudly enough for the whole group to hear. Looking up at them, he pulled out the bag of trail foods and tossed it in their direction. One scampered forward and caught it, then began excitedly inspecting the contents and passing them among his companions. "What is this thing that I need to know?" Solomon asked, looking back at the man again.

The man looked at the other beggars questioningly. One of them motioned for him to speak. Turning back to Solomon, he straightened, and declared, "My lord, the ancient landmarks in this place are in need of redemption. My family has land here, as do most of us—good land. When our fathers first came to this place, they discovered that a large portion of it was unplantable. Down below," he motioned toward the valley, "is a marsh, unfit for planting or for grazing animals, while up above," he motioned toward the hills, "it is too dry to plant—there are no springs. But in between, the land produces like Eden itself. Our fathers set the landmarks so that each family would have plantable land. But in our generation, the good land has been purchased for the years remaining until Jubilee, leaving my family only with that land which is unfit for planting."

"The land has been purchased?" Solomon asked, his instincts as a judge rising up. "By whom?"

The man looked around nervously, up and down the street. Then he leaned forward and whispered, "By a man named Baal Hamon. He is a rich and powerful man who lives in this area."

"And what of Hamon's own land?"

"That is just it, my lord. Hamon is not an Israelite, though he poses as one. He is entitled to no land here, the truth be known. But he has claimed our land here as his own—purchased it."

"But Jubilee is some years off. And crops are prospering. Can no one redeem the land?"

The man shook his head. "They cannot, my lord. Hamon bought the years at a reduced price during a famine, but will only allow redemption at full price. No one here can raise that much."

Solomon shook his head. What kind of foreigner could wield such power over Israelites? It could not happen without the cooperation of Israelite judges, who must have something to gain from it all. It appeared that there was real work for him to do in this town after all.

"But, please, my lord," the man spoke again, moving in close, "you did not hear this from me!"

The street was now almost devoid of travelers. It had cleared out rather quickly. The sound of music could be heard emanating from an open doorway up the street.

Solomon leaned down, and then pressed the loaf of bread he had purchased into the beggar's chest, who took it, and looked up questioningly. "Jared," Solomon said in a low voice, "I have seen fools riding horses, while princes walk on the ground. Be assured I will not through indiscreet talk multiply the undeserved troubles of a worthy man. I am only staying in this place for a short while, and I pray that God gives you justice and success. But this I charge you to remember: There is justice in Israel if taken before a high enough court. Hamon may be powerful here, but there are powers greater than he."

"I believe that, my lord," the man answered. "But justice comes slowly to a remote place like this. Until then, we must guard our steps."

"Yes, of course," Solomon replied, pausing to stare at the man most peculiarly—an expression that did not go unnoticed by Jared. In truth, Solomon was fighting off a strong instinct to act on the situation immediately.

Looking up at the group of beggars, Solomon said, "I will see you again." He spurred his donkey forward, and the group chorused gratitude as he rode off.

Chapter 12

The path below Abishag's feet was black as she hastened toward the city, its buildings a dark cluster of shapes amid twinkling torchlights. The trail had become mostly vacant of passersby. She asked a few travelers on the trail if they had seen a limping traveler, but none had. She pulled her garments closer as she neared the city gate. A couple of graybeards lingered there, though it looked as though they were preparing to depart.

"Excuse me, my lords," she asked, approaching them quickly and bowing.

The men turned to look at her, surprised. One bent down and looked at her closely in the half-light.

"Abishag?"

"Yes, my lord . . . Obed?"

"Yes, daughter. What are you doing down here at this time of night? Should you not be getting home?"

"Yes, my lord, but I'm looking for someone, a wounded stranger who is staying in our house. He may be lost or in need. Have you been here all day?"

"Most of the day, yes, but I have not seen any wounded strangers."

"Hmm," she said, becoming more worried. "No one?—no

one at all?" she asked again.

"Well, yes," he said then, remembering, "there *was* a stranger who passed by earlier—a shepherd, I suppose—someone I had not seen before, but he did not appear to be wounded."

"Well, this fellow is not a shepherd," she said, "and he would have been limping badly."

"It's hard to limp while riding a donkey," he replied.

She frowned, remembering the sound of the rider earlier in the day, and the hoof tracks at their home. Could it have been a donkey?

"He was riding a donkey? Could you describe him?" she asked.

"Well, now, that was some hours ago, and I had not expected to be asked, but it seems to me that he was dressed in a long woolen cloak, brown or gray, had a light-colored turban, a healthy beard, and a shepherd's staff. That's about all I remember."

She considered the information. It sounded at least partially right.

"Well, which way did he go?"

The man pointed down the street. "He either went through town, or he is still in town. He did not come back out this way, that much I know."

She knew it was unlikely that a traveler would have continued on that late in the day. The city of Jezreel was at least another three miles away. So, if it was her visitor the graybeard had seen, he was probably still in the city somewhere.

"Well, I believe I should go on and seek him. He may need help," she said.

"Abishag, you be careful," the kindly old man said. "You know that the men are drinking by now. You really shouldn't be out at all."

"I will, my lord, and thank you, my lord."

She left bowing. The old man looked after her as she made

her way down the street, the dark form of a lone woman looking very much out of place in the brooding atmosphere that infused the developing evening.

****

Solomon stopped at the door where he had heard the music and peered inside from his mount. Though it was a drinking room, odds were it also kept a cooking iron. Food helped drinking men stay longer. Now that Solomon had given all of his food away, he would either have to buy something, or wait and trouble Abishag and the widow later. He swung off the donkey and hobbled into the entrance, using his shepherd's rod as a cane. The place seemed busy already, with drinks being served up to a bustling crowd of young and old men. He found a place to sit near the door. The owner of the establishment spotted him and motioned to a young woman to go over and serve him. She sauntered over.

She was a pretty little maiden, short, but also bold, and not afraid to look a man right in the eye—a girl who rarely blushed. "And what are we drinking tonight?" she asked him, omitting the courtesy of a greeting.

Solomon measured the daring little maiden who addressed him more casually than he had ever been talked to by a woman in his life.

"Well, daughter," he said, "I am not drinking. I am just here for a meal, and I will be on my way. What do you serve?"

She eyed him skeptically. The girl had been well-trained in how to coax money out of passing travelers.

"Oh, we got lots of good food here," she said, grinning, "but you know where you are, don't you? You are in Shunem, home of the best vineyards in the land of Israel. You don't want to pass through our town without a taste of Israel's finest—especially since it is our courtesy, no charge at all. Simply choose what food you want, and I'll bring you samples of two of our finest wines to go with it. You tell me which one you like best."

It was a clever ploy, and likely to work in most cases. But

155

Solomon remembered his Nazarite vow. Even if he had wanted to taste the wine, he could not.

"You are most hospitable," Solomon replied.

The girl smiled. "My father has determined that we treat those who come through our doors as friends."

Solomon looked around the noisy room. "Friends, you say?"

"So my father regards them."

"Daughter, are you married?" Solomon suddenly asked.

She looked at him strangely. "No. Why?"

His peculiar gaze settled over her like a garment, a gaze under which she suddenly felt uncertain.

"Maiden, surely I am confused. You enjoy the company of a room full of friends every evening, and yet you remain unmarried? If the saloonkeeper thinks every drunk a friend, why is his daughter wed to none of them?"

She opened her mouth, then hesitated. The moment suddenly felt surreal.

"You are clever," she replied, then glanced back at her father nervously.

"And if you do not convince me to accept your wine, your kind father may have words with you later," he observed.

He saw recognition flash over her face.

"Therefore, in order that I might return your friendship, I oblige you to bring me the wine, and I will pay for it. But drink it I cannot, for I am under the Nazarite vow."

"I see," she said, pursing her lips, but with a silent thank-you in her eyes.

"If you would be so kind, along with your excellent wine, I would be most grateful if you would bring me a dish of vegetables, and some fowl if you have it," he said.

The girl studied him, then nodded.

156

"As you wish, my lord."

She disappeared into the back.

Solomon scanned the crowded room. It was a busy place for a town this size, especially on a work night. Some of the men had already downed several drinks and were becoming noisy. The atmosphere was rougher than one would normally expect in a small quiet village.

Solomon was feeling tired. He just wanted to get his meal and be on his way. He closed his eyes and leaned his head against the wooden bench back behind him, resting. The conversations around him suddenly sprang to life. There was all the normal jesting and small talk you might hear among working men, but one particular conversation nearby caught his attention. Two men were conversing carefully in low, business-like tones. One of them sounded older than the other.

"We have been through all of this before, Jockshan," said the young voice. "How many times do we have to rewrite this deal? Or did we ever have a deal?"

"Of course we do," replied the elder. "How long have we known each other? Your father was my friend. I was there the day he was married to your mother. I delivered you. If you cannot trust me, who can you trust?"

"Yes, and you know my father's true condition better than anyone. How much longer does he have?—a year, six months, what?" the younger asked.

"Your father will pass when it is his time, and you stand to make his whole estate yours. You need not be impatient. Extending the payments for a few more months will not destroy you," came the reply.

The voice of the older man carried more strain than that of the younger, a situation which sounded a bit unbecoming to Solomon's ears. He opened his eyes and glanced over casually at the two men. They were leaning forward, locked in conversation at a corner table. So this was Jockshan the physician, but who was this powerful young man who seemed to have the advantage on

157

the wealthy older professional? Solomon sized him up. He could tell that he was tall, even though he was seated. Immaculately dressed, and very well groomed, he looked a bit like a prince, such as those Solomon had often entertained from faraway lands. He was probably close in age to Solomon himself, and he had an authoritative air about him. Though the present conversation was important to the young man, it was more important to his companion, and the former's body language revealed the casual confidence that Solomon had seen often among the wealthy.

"I am not concerned with what will destroy me," the young prince replied, "but with what is of benefit to me. Tell me, if we extend the terms again, what do I gain? Surely a businessman such as yourself would not expect me to do this for nothing."

"I am not a businessman," Jockshan growled. "I am a physician. I serve humanity, and it is not for myself, but for the benefit of many, that I act."

"I suspect that you are offering me the fool's bargain now to keep the land in your possession until after harvest, after which time, we may not have a deal at all," the young man replied.

"And why shouldn't it stay in our hands until after harvest?!" The elder man's voice was rising. Suddenly, he broke off as the serving girl walked by to place Solomon's meal in front of him. Solomon began to eat, still listening carefully to the conversation.

"And why shouldn't it?" the man repeated, this time in more hushed tones. "My family, and many others, cultivated, watered, fertilized, and pruned all summer. These diligent Israelites deserve to reap the profits of their own harvest!"

"And I don't have a right to the payments we agreed upon?" the other asked. "Come now, Jockshan. Everyone knows that I am not in the habit of selling land. I buy land. I only sold these fields to you because of the terms to which you agreed. If you had offered me these terms in the beginning, there would have been no deal. If now, at this late date, you want to modify everything to my detriment, you must offer me sufficient compensation, to make up the difference."

"I only bought from you to return to born Israelites land that was rightfully theirs to begin with!" hissed the elder man.

"And on this point we disagree, as usual," replied the young man. "So how do we proceed from here, things being as they are?"

There was a pause in the conversation. The elder man was thinking hard, stroking his well-kept beard, eyes staring at the floor. The young man leaned back in his seat and took a sip of his wine. Then, almost casually, he said, "What about the fields on the west hill?"

The elder man's head snapped up to look at him, his eyes narrowing.

"You know very well that is my brother's land. I only hold it in trust for him. I am not authorized to sell it to you, or to anyone else," he replied in a low, level voice.

"You are the kinsman redeemer, are you not?" replied the young man. "The land is yours to do with as you wish until an heir is raised up, which does not seem . . . imminent."

As he spoke these words, the slightest trace of a smile crossed his lips. The elder man was sullenly silent, not unaware of the insult.

"Besides, I am not asking you to sell anything," the younger continued. "I am just exploring ways in which we might break this impasse. Your payments are secure, I have no doubt."

"Of course my payments are secure!" Jockshan replied.

"Well, then," the young man responded with an air of conclusion, "that being the case, for what cause do you hesitate to put the west hill up as security?" Then, pausing for a beat, he continued, ". . . Or are you not as certain of your means as you suggest?"

The elder man's quandary was evident to Solomon. Apparently, he had concocted an arrangement to buy back land to return it to the rightful owners, both for his own family, and for some others. He was counting on a profitable harvest to raise the funds to pay for it. But now he was running low on money. If he did not agree to the young man's demands, he faced the proposition of losing the land he presently held, along with the profit from the harvest for which everyone had toiled. But if he put up his dead brother's estate as security, he risked losing that also, if for some reason he could not keep up the payments. Cases just such as this were what made Solomon's own court so important in Israel, but for now, he would have to let this situation run its course. He was not here to judge; he was here to test a potential queen, unknown. There would be time for rendering judgments later.

Finally, the elder man spoke.

"I will give you my answer in the morning," he said, rising up to leave the room. The young man nodded almost imperceptibly, staring him down with confidence.

"Very well," he replied. "And thank you for the drink."

"What?"

"You did invite me here, did you not?"

"Oh, yes, yes, of course," Jockshan replied, and shuffled over to pay the owner before quickly making his way out the door, not stopping to look back at the young prince.

The serving girl was standing before Solomon.

"You finished that off like a king! Are you sure you don't want to try that drink? You look like you could use it." she said, noting Solomon's disgusted expression.

"It would be of no benefit to me even if I did," he said. "Wine is a mocker and strong drink a brawler, and he who is deceived thereby is not wise."

"Hmm, you are a poet too!"

Solomon chuckled. "Yes, I suppose I do enjoy a good verse from time to time. How much do I owe you?"

"Six silver Gerahs."

Solomon reached down into his money pouch. Ah, he had forgotten again. Nothing there but gold. Gold weights were at least five times the value of silver. He was not used to paying for his own things like this, and not having smaller apportions was becoming inconvenient. He held the gold piece out in his hand to her, low, where only she could see it.

"Could you break this? It's all I have."

She looked at the gold piece, then eyed the strange shepherd up and down.

"I'll see," she said, and took the piece, concealing it in her hand while discreetly walking over to where her father sat.

Solomon watched her open her hand and converse with him briefly across the room. Then the owner pointed back over in Solomon's direction. The girl walked toward him, but then turned, and went to speak to the young man who had been sitting with Jockshan. He saw her point over to where he was sitting. The young man glanced at him, and then back at the gold piece. Solomon could not hear the girl's words, but the young man's reply was audible.

"Certainly, I have it, but of course you know my usual fee," he said.

"But his whole meal was only six Gerahs," she protested, loud enough to be heard now. "Your fee would cost more than that!"

"Well, I suppose this man gets a free meal then," he declared loudly enough for Solomon to hear, glancing over at him and giving him a wink.

Several other patrons in the room were starting to notice the exchange.

"Excuse me," Solomon said, rising to his feet.

The girl looked over at him.

"I will pay the fee. I am sorry. I should have come better prepared."

Both the girl and the young man stared at him in silence.

"Truly, it is only proper," Solomon said. "How much is the fee?"

She started to walk over toward him. Abruptly, the young man stopped her, taking her by the arm.

"No!" he blurted, then paused. "No," he repeated more calmly. "I will cover this man's meal…and the fee."

He looked expectantly at Solomon.

Solomon managed a half bow, keeping his weight on his good foot.

"Thank you, my lord," he said with simple dignity, nodding at the young prince. Turning to the girl, he said, "And thank you, daughter. The quality of your wine surpassed your every claim, and the dish you served was a delight."

The room was suddenly silent. The dignity of his comment spoken from full standing height had commanded the attention of everyone. The girl blushed, and slipped the coin back into his hand. He turned to make his way out, the eyes of every occupant now following him in curious silence. He limped to the door, bracing himself on his staff, then turned back to bow at his inquisitive audience. After he closed the door behind him, curious murmurings rumbled through the room.

Solomon stepped into the cool night air, pausing to take a deep breath of it, his mind reflecting on what he had learned. The sky was dark and clear, awaiting a late-rising moon. He glanced up at the stars, pondering. It had been an illuminating day, with respect to the unusual events playing out in this small, rural town of Shunem.

He also was beginning to learn something about himself: He did not blend well. Though he was trying to avoid drawing attention to himself, it was proving difficult. His every simple action turned into a scene of some sort. Could he truly remain unknown? He realized he would be discovered eventually. Someone who could identify him would pass through town. But perhaps he could delay the inevitable for what time he needed, simply by not declaring himself. How much time would that strategy buy him? It would have to be enough.

It was beyond time to be getting back now. Leaning on his

shepherd's staff, he swung up onto his donkey and headed up the
street toward the gate.

Chapter 13

Abishag was starting to have serious misgivings. She had never been the sort to be out on the streets at night. For one thing, she had always risen early to long days of labor, making a good night's sleep important. But more than that, a woman who made a habit of being seen out late could garner a reputation—one that she did not need to encourage, especially not in this place. Her honor was already questionable in the eyes of some—that, she knew. Her own brothers were little help.

She moved quickly through the barren streets, peeking up and down the alleys for some sign of the traveler. Not a soul was out walking around, and the only place where activity was visible was in and around the drinking rooms. She considered looking there, but she did not really want to venture into such places. If she felt uncomfortable in the streets at night, she would feel completely lost in those grubby caves. Besides, if she did find him there, what would she say, anyway? She circled around, giving the drinking rooms a wide berth. If he was in one of them, she probably did not want to find him anyway.

Perhaps he was not coming back at all, and had just used their house as a place to rest and recover. Was he a vagabond?—or a man on the run? Would he be found down here, drunk? Several times she seriously considered giving up a search that was quickly appearing foolish, and hastening home. But Shunem was a small

165

town; she could at least check down all the main streets. At the far end of town was an inn. She knew the owners; she could inquire of them. She would go that far, and if there were still no sign of him, she would go home. Wanting to save time, she took a shortcut through a narrow alley with high walls.

Suddenly, the ground crackled underneath her feet. Broken pottery. She glanced up at the building next to her. Perhaps something had fallen off the roof? It was sharp. She slowed down and carefully stepped out of the mess, studying the ground in the half-light. She heard laughter ahead and looked up to see three men rounding the corner and coming up the alley toward her. They were visibly drunk, jostling and shoving each other as they moved down the dark alley.

"Hey, what's this?" one of them said, pointing in the direction where Abishag had stopped still. They continued toward her. She felt a surge of discomfort, looking around to see if there were any other people nearby, any doorways or places to turn. There weren't. She would have to keep walking forward, or turn around and go back. Either way, she was plainly in their view. She moved forward, close to the wall, keeping her eyes down as if she had not seen them. The men were in no particular hurry, having no real place to be other than where they were right now. They sauntered down the alley, talking and laughing loudly.

Abishag recognized one of the voices. It was Hamon's younger brother, Caleh. He had been born a child of privilege, enjoying the benefits of a wealthy family, while the responsibilities were carried by his brother. He was generally harmless, but was known to be reckless when drunk.

As the men neared her, she heard them slurring the words of a common drinking song—*Who knows what we're looking for? We seen the wall, now where's the door?* Abishag knew very well what it meant. She quickened her pace to rush past them.

"Hey, there—what's the big hurry?"

One of them stepped in front of her, blocking her path along the wall. There was nothing to do but face them.

"Yeah, where you goin' so fast?" another said.

"I'm sorry," Abishag replied. "I'm in a bit of a hurry. I'm looking for someone."

"You didn't seem to be going nowhere a minute ago," said one.

"Look no further," declared another. "I'm right here!" He chortled, obviously pleased with himself.

Abishag kept her head down, discouraging interaction. She could not think of anything to say. *This is bad!* She could not believe she was here. She closed her eyes, wishing she were home. What could she even say? The men were too drunk to reason with, and seeing a woman at night with a veil on was often an indication that she was out soliciting. She knew prostitutes liked to dress in "virgin" attire; it was part of their act. The only difference was that, under the veil, a prostitute would tint her eyelids and lips with coloring, demonstrating that she did in fact intend to be seen, while a virgin would not. But in this dark alley, it would be impossible to tell the difference.

"I'm sorry, you don't understand," she protested. "I really *am* looking for someone!"

"Who?" one demanded.

"Well, I don't know . . . Have—have you seen him? He's tall and he, he . . ." She broke off, realizing how bad it was sounding. "Caleh!" She blurted. "Remember me?" She looked up at him for the first time.

He took a step closer.

"Hey, yes, I know who you are! You're that widow's daughter, Abby-rag? Right?"

"What is it, Caleh?" one of his companions asked. "Is she a door?"

"Don't know," Caleh replied. "Always wondered, though. And she sure don't look like no wall!" he continued, allowing himself a long, shameless look up and down Abishag's figure, draped though it was in her full-length workday garment.

The other two guffawed loudly.

"Maybe we should go somewhere and talk about this. I don't think you're gonna find anyone else out here tonight, so how about coming with us?"

"No, really, I must be going . . ." she said, taking a quick step forward to try to squeeze by.

"I really don't think you must," one of the men said, grabbing her by the arm. She could smell the alcohol hot on his breath. "Like Caleh said, we need to talk about this, right?" he asked, smiling back and forth from Abishag to his companion.

Then the man began to tug at her veil, leaning in close to get a better look at her face. Abishag struggled.

"If you wish to speak with this virgin, you must first talk to me!"

The voice sounded suddenly from behind the men. It was deep and authoritative, startling them as much by the fact that they had not heard him approach as by his tone. It was as though a chief judge from the city gate had arrived. The men wheeled around to see the silhouette of a tall, hooded figure on a donkey, a long, thick shepherd's staff in his hand. Instinctively, the man let go of Abishag's arm as though he had been caught in a crime.

Noticing this, Solomon spoke again before anyone else reacted. "Abishag, step this way, please."

Instinctively, Abishag obeyed. There was immense authority in the man's voice. She was past the man who had grabbed her and back behind the donkey before anyone else had moved.

Caleh peered curiously up at the hooded stranger. His features could not be seen at all. Gaining some composure, he replied, "Wait, we meant her no harm, but I don't believe I know who you are."

"I don't believe you do," Solomon agreed.

"You . . . are you a shepherd?" he asked, observing the staff.

"I am this woman's brother. I have come to take her home, and if you wish to speak to her, you must speak to me first . . . in the daytime. That is all you need to know," Solomon replied, then said to Abishag, "Mount up, sister; let's be going." Abishag deftly hopped up behind Solomon, grasping tightly around his waist for support. In the process, she kicked his injured foot slightly, and Solomon winced.

Suddenly, Caleh was emboldened. His surprise had given way to his need to save face before his friends.

"Now, wait just a minute! I know her brothers!" he declared. "And you are not one of them! Do you know who I am?"

Solomon had seen Abishag's situation and acted instinctively. But now, he was becoming aware that he was, in fact, acting alone, without the backup he so often took for granted. There was no one else here to enforce his wishes. Doing so himself against these three men would be difficult in full health, let alone with a broken leg. There was no authority here other than that which he himself could muster.

"Do you know who *I* am?" Solomon returned the question, keeping his tone rich with authority.

"You are the woman's brother," came a calm voice from behind him. "And it is time for you to be getting home. Caleh, step back. There is no need for trouble tonight."

Everyone turned to look. Solomon recognized the young prince he had seen in the drinking room.

"Hamon!" Caleh exclaimed. "We were just passing by. There is no trouble here—we were just talking to her."

Hamon continued to walk casually, right into the middle of the group, Caleh and his two companions suddenly acting submissive.

"Yes, of course, there is no trouble here," Hamon said calmly. "Abishag's brother will be visiting our area for a while. We are honored to show him the hospitality he deserves. I just bought him a meal." Then he turned to Solomon. "Please be on your way, my friend, and forgive the impertinence of my brother. He is young."

It was a night of strange moments. When had Solomon ever

been in a position where he needed rescue by the hand of someone wielding a higher authority than he? But under these unique circumstances, that was exactly what was happening. There was nothing to do but accept it.

"All is forgiven," Solomon replied. "I have younger brothers also. My lord, I find myself in your debt for the second time this evening. Shalom." Then he turned and spurred the donkey up the street.

Solomon had not noticed until this moment that Abishag was trembling, and still gripping him hard. They rounded a corner and proceeded down the street for several blocks in silence.

"I don't think you are in danger of falling off, sister."

Abishag let out a short tension-relieving gush of air, half-laugh.

"Yes, um, no, of course," she replied, loosening her death grip just a bit.

They traveled on in silence for a short while. He could tell she was still terrified.

"You were down here looking for me?" he asked.

"Well, yes. I knew you were injured and I thought I would try the inn, and then . . ." Her voice shook.

Solomon noticed.

Atmosphere . . . a little conversation to calm the nerves . . .

"It is wise that you avoid coming down here at night—you were quite brave. Your kindness to a stranger is uncommon."

"Yes, well, I can see that you seem to be able to take care of yourself," she replied.

Solomon chuckled. It was, in fact, the first time in his life that he had been required to take care of himself. And had the young prince not appeared . . . well, he hated to think about how events might have transpired.

"With a bit of luck, I muddle through. But there is one thing I need your help with, if you don't mind."

170

"Of course, my lord, but what could I do for you?" she asked.

"I came down here in search of a doctor to set my leg, but I was not able to get in. I purchased some supplies, and I need you to do it for me."

"Set the bone? I would if I could, but I don't know how to do that."

"I know how it is done. You need only do what I explain to you."

"You . . . know how to set a bone?"

"Yes, I know that, and a few other things. It's not too difficult, once you understand the principle. Any maiden with the courage to come down to town alone at night to rescue a stranger would certainly have what it takes to set a bone."

At that she laughed naturally.

"I guess it was a bit foolish, wasn't it?"

"Yes, but it was also quite noble. I won't hold it against you. Just don't try it again. I wouldn't really want to fight three men with a broken foot if I could help it."

They continued to converse as they moved up the path in the moonlight, gaining altitude. The torchlights of the town in the peaceful valley below diminished into a ring of twinkling lights, like a leaf floating on a black pool. Abishag suddenly felt a twinge of embarrassment. This was the second time in twenty-four hours that she found herself traveling in close contact with this stranger. She had held onto him to begin with because she was frightened, but now that her fear had passed, she realized it was no longer necessary.

"I should get off and walk now."

"If you wish," Solomon replied, "but we will be home before too long, and we have come this far. It is no insult to me, and your honor is not in question."

"Just the same, I think I'll walk now."

Solomon pulled up to let her dismount, charmed by her

modesty. It was a welcome change from how he was normally treated by eligible women. He had no desire to talk her out of what her conscience required.

"I should walk and let you ride," he kidded. "You have had a hard night."

Now she laughed as she dismounted. "No, thank you. I want to get home before sunrise."

"Well, maybe some other time then."

"Yes."

Her mysterious visitor had a way about him. He was exceedingly polite to her, but not gushing, emanating a simple dignity that seemed to calm the soul. He was perfectly at ease with himself, as though he needed nothing at all. He could make her laugh, but without invoking silliness, treating her with all the respect due a queen. Did he not realize she was just a worthless peasant girl?—or did he treat everyone that way. She was not used to such treatment, and it inspired a reflex of trust, despite her hardly knowing him.

She reflected how he had so effortlessly intervened in her behalf, a quickly building reservoir of respect for him attending the memory. One thing she knew for certain. This was no wanderer, no vagabond. He carried himself with too much dignity. This was a man of honor. How could he move so effortlessly between the steely confidence of authority, such as when he addressed the men in the street, and such gentle kindness when he talked with her? And such perfect control! It revealed a startling depth of character. She suddenly felt completely safe, as though not a power in the world could harm her. How did he emit that magical aura that could even spill over onto her in such a short time? It was curious. She walked along next to the donkey, pondering.

"What would you have done if Hamon had not shown up?"

His silence lingered, and she glanced up.

"So that was Baal Hamon? The man you told me about yesterday?"

"Yes," she said, being reminded of the conversation they had had in the vineyard. "That was Baal Hamon, the Younger, the heir of all his father's estate."

"He seemed kind enough to me."

She sighed deeply. "He has a talent for that. Hamon can make people think that he . . . well, there was a time . . ." she began, her voice trailing off.

Solomon glanced over.

"Hamon? Not Baal Hamon?"

She blinked.

"Oh—well, we grew up together in this place, Hamon—I mean, *Baal* Hamon—and I. Sometimes I remember how he used to be. Sometimes I still hope for him, but . . ."

Solomon continued looking ahead as her silence lingered. Chancing a glance, he found her eyes had drifted far away.

"And now?"

"Now?" she repeated. "Hamon is kind only when it suits his interest. If he treats you kindly, beware. This much I know."

The clopping of the donkey's feet on the trail echoed against the nearby hills, while the now fully-risen moon was bright enough to draw odd shadows from the travelers' feet. Each of them were walking on in silent contemplation.

"Did he really buy you a meal?" she asked.

Solomon chuckled. "Yes, he did, but only because I shamed him into it."

Abishag pursed her lips in private amusement. Hamon was not prone to being shamed into anything. But from what she had seen of this stranger so far, if anyone could do it, he could.

"Well, then, I'm sure he deserved it, though I'm not sure how you could have accomplished such a thing."

They were nearing the farm now. A light was visible inside the doorway; the widow, Abelah, was awake.

"A man cannot be shamed save there be something in him to be ashamed of," Solomon replied. "Then it is just a matter of revealing what is already there."

"But can not a man be shamed wrongly? When he has done no wrong?"

"Then it is not shame, but condemnation. Condemnation comes from the outside, but shame comes from within."

The thought descended into her mind, turning and flickering there, glowing with sage truth.

"You say the most interesting things," she replied finally, her eyes now almost unseeing of the path beneath her feet.

"Only interesting to those in whom truth can find a place to rest. The wise and the fool are alike in this: Folly is drawn to the fool because folly is in his heart. In the same way, the wise attract wisdom, because wisdom is already resident in them."

Abishag glanced up. His face was turned toward her but was lost in the shadow of his turban, leaving his expression to her imagination.

"I think that was a compliment."

"It was."

****

As Solomon and Abishag neared the house, the widow flew out the door to meet them. She was not used to having her only daughter out at night and began calling from the porch as soon as she crossed the threshold toward them.

"Abishag! Daughter, oh, you naughty girl!—how you have made me suffer! I cannot remember a time when I fretted so for you! I have had you everywhere from lost, to kidnapped, to drowned in the swamp! Is everything all right?" she asked, casting suspicious glances at the stranger on the donkey.

"Yes, Mother," Abishag assured her.

The widow's head turned quickly back to her daughter. She appeared completely at ease, as though she had just been out for a walk on a spring day. The tall man with her wore a similar expression.

"Your daughter is quite brave," he said to Abelah. "She took great pains to bring me back here safely."

"He is the brave one, Mother," Abishag whispered, brushing by through the door to make a place ready for her injured guest to sit down.

Abelah looked up at the man on the donkey. "I have prepared the guest room out back," the widow commented, gesturing toward a small shack across the yard. "You must be very tired, my lord."

"I am, thank you, but there is one important piece of business to attend to before I retire," Solomon said, swinging awkwardly down off the donkey. "I am afraid your local doctor is overly busy, and your daughter has graciously volunteered to set the bone in my leg."

"What?!" the widow exclaimed.

From the doorway, Abishag exhaled a laugh. "I *agreed* to do it, Mother, and he assures me that I can, so I will."

The smile that swelled in Solomon's mind was wider than the one on his lips. He hobbled into the room and up onto the stool she had prepared, leaning his back against the wall of the cabin and reaching into his clothing for the vine rods.

"You will need several strips of cloth, each about a cubit in length," Solomon said.

The widow began scurrying around, digging through some containers. Abishag knelt down in front of Solomon, taking his foot in her hands. Her headdress was still wrapped around it. Abelah was not finding anything.

"Let's use this," Abishag said, carefully unwrapping his foot. Her mother looked over at her strangely.

"I have others," she explained, looking up at Solomon and smiling. He had already worn it all day, and she could think of no more noble use for one of her veils than to heal the foot of this dignified stranger.

"It will be perfect," Solomon replied.

Abelah's motherly intuition caught a whiff of something. Some indiscernible but not unpleasant commerce must have passed between her daughter and this man in the short trip back from town. She ceased her searching and crossed the room, reaching up into a cabinet.

"Very well, then, but I'm sure you will want to have some wine first," she said, considering the pain the man was about to endure.

"That will not be necessary, dear mother," Solomon said flatly, a bit of authority creeping into his voice. The woman stopped in mid-motion, glancing back at him curiously. She saw that the resolve in his eyes matched the tone in his voice. Instead, she crossed back over and found a seat.

Abishag had cut the headdress into strips and laid them out on the floor before her.

"Ready to proceed?" Solomon asked.

She nodded.

He explained to her how to use the rods, laying them out before her in a row. They would encircle the ankle and the strips would tie them in place. Rods would be crimped in the front to follow the contour of his foot.

"Now here is the difficult part," he said. "Get me something to write on, please."

Abelah found a flat piece of patch-cloth and some charcoal and handed them to him. Solomon sketched out a picture of an ankle and foot, showing the bones inside. Then he drew a line across, indicating where the break would be found.

"Here is the break, as best as I can tell. You must set the bones so that they mate. They will naturally incline to that position, but you must apply firm pressure to assure that there is no gap between them. Only then can the rods be set. Be firm, and be deliberate. It is better to take what time you need to be sure than to set the bones incorrectly. Now, please hand me one of those rods."

She handed him one, looking at him curiously. Solomon leaned back and held the rod close to his mouth. "You may proceed now," he said, taking the rod in his teeth and biting down.

Abishag started to perspire. She leaned forward and gently took his foot in her hands, chancing a glance up at his face. He merely nodded. She wrapped one of the strips around his leg just below the knee, tying it off snugly. Then she carefully began feeling up the ankle until she found the point indicated on the sketch. With her other hand, she felt down the upper bone, until she had come to almost the same place. As she neared it, she saw his hand clenching into a tight, white fist.

"That is it," Solomon said, still biting on the rod. His voice was completely calm, but the pupils of his eyes were dilating, and beads of sweat were forming on his forehead.

Abishag looked back down at her hands, hoping they were not trembling. Then she began to squeeze, harder, harder, until she was sure she could feel the bones. Solomon was absolutely still and silent. Her mother watched, hand over her mouth, eyes wide. Abishag applied more direct pressure in the spot, feeling the foot rise up ever so slightly as she did. The bones felt like they had mated. She slid her knee under the foot to support it there.

"Good," Solomon whispered.

Then she took four of the rods, and inserted them into the strip of cloth below his knee, one on the front, one on the back, and one on each side. She concentrated hard to keep her hands from shaking. Then she took another strip and encircled the ankle and the rods below the break, tying the rods together snugly. Once these were in place, she began filling in all the spaces in between with more rods, and when the ankle was completely covered, she tied the rest of the strips around the bundle, spacing them evenly. She was amazed at the self-control of the man as she worked. He did not so much as let out a peep, though his pain was obviously intense. Eventually, he removed the rod from his teeth. It was bitten nearly in half.

"That was not so bad now, was it? You have a fine talent," he remarked, his voice ever so slightly out of normal timbre, a brief smile on his lips. She sighed heavily and dropped her hands on her lap, looking up at him.

"I have only done what you told me," she replied, "and I hope it was right."

"It was," he assured her, moving to rise. She quickly got up to help him.

"And now, if you would be so kind as to show me the guest room, I believe I should retire."

The women escorted him out across the yard to the small room, where a bed was situated among sparse furnishings. Solomon smiled at the quaint little place.

"This will be splendid," he said. "Thank you for your hospitality. Sleep well, and I will see you in the morning."

"Yes, yes, shalom. If you need anything else, I'll be right over here . . ." Abishag said, lingering in the awkward silence following her last available comment. "Yes, well, shalom." she repeated.

Solomon looked back over his shoulder at her as he seated himself on the humble bed, pausing just a moment to deposit a glance directly into her large, dark eyes.

"Shalom, sister."

A shiver went up her spine. She closed the door, lingering just beyond it. Her own brothers sometimes addressed her as "sister," but she had no idea the term could be draped with such gentle kindness. She felt strangely warm. Taking a deep breath, she let it out with an involuntary shudder.

Then she drifted back toward her bed, an almost fragrant sensation of awe hovering above and around her like a cloud.

She lay awake for a long time.

Continued in Book Two:

The Shepherd King

Available from

www.secretwineonline.com

End Notes

[1] Endnote 1, page 3, Solomon the 4th born of David and Bathsheba

The suggestion that Solomon was not the firstborn of Bathsheba is unexpected by some readers, because in the narrative passage where David's first son of Bathsheba dies, it sounds like Solomon is born right away, and is the first surviving son of David and Bathsheba. (2 Sam. 12:24) I agree, it does appear that way in the Biblical narrative. However, in three separate Biblical genealogies, Solomon is named the 4th of Bathsheba, behind Shimea, Shobab, and Nathan. (2 Samuel 5:14, 1 Chronicles 3:5, 1 Chronicles 14:3, 4) Anytime two scriptures seem to be at dissonance, it is important to have some sensible and consistent rule by which to resolve the conflict. In this case, the question is not doctrinally complex, but simply a question of birth order. A narrative passage seems to be contradicting a genealogy. How is this to be resolved? I suggest it is a mistake to give a narrative priority over a genealogy in determining birth order, because a genealogy is a legal instrument, a separate document designed for the *very purpose* of establishing parentage and birth order. Genealogies had to be both clear and correct for the proper conveyance of inheritances and birthright privileges, among other things. A narrative has broader purposes: instructive, homiletical, and historical. This broader purpose does not demand the same technical exactitude required of a genealogy on the subject of birth order. (If such questions were demanded of the narrative, one could argue Cain was the son of Adam, Gen. 4:1, and Abraham was not the father of Ishmael. *"And he said, Take now thy son, thine ONLY SON Isaac, whom thou lovest, and get thee into the land of Moriah; and offer him there for a burnt offering upon one of the mountains which I will tell thee of."* (Genesis 22:2, KJV).

If we examine the method of the chronicler in 1 Chronicles, we can discern his rule: he consistently names sons in order of birth. Also, this is a very detailed genealogy. In chapter one, we find his lists even more complete than the first patriarchal genealogy of Genesis Ch. 10-11. Therefore, there were other genealogical documents available to this chronicler at a very late date, even more detailed than those included in the Genesis record. No genealogy in the Bible is longer or more complete than that of the first nine chapters of 1 Chronicles. Additional names are included, perhaps to demonstrate the authoritative nature of this list, and the completeness of the sources this chronicler had to work with. In verses 24-27, he then *summarizes* the line of Shem to Abraham, omitting all sons that are not in the direct line. This demonstrates that what this chronicler includes, and chooses not to include, are for specific purposes, not for lack of information.

Following that verse, a complete legal genealogy begins. This includes all of the sons of Ishmael, (starting at verse 28) and then of Esau, (starting at verse 34) not just those leading to a pre-determined person. (as in Abraham, above) In taking these lines, the chronicler lists first the lineages who are NOT part of the messianic line, as is consistent throughout the scripture. All twelve of Ismael's sons are named, and all five of Esau's, ending in the eleven dukes of Edom. (1:51-54)

Then in 1 Ch. 2, the chronicler backs up to begin again with the line of Jacob. He names the six sons of Leah in the order she bore them, (Reuben, Simeon, Levi, Judah, Issachar and Zebulun)

Then he lists the sons attributed to Rachel and her handmaid, Dan, Joseph, Benjamin, and Naphtali.

The account of Jacob's family ends with the two sons of Leah's handmaid Zilpah, Gad and Asher.

It should be noticed that in *no case* are a wife's (or handmaid's) sons named out of birth order. Rachel bore Joseph and Benjamin in that order. Bilhah bore Dan and Naphtali in that order. Zilpah bore Gad and Asher in that order. And Leah bore Reuben, Simeon, Levi, Judah, Issachar and Zebulun in that order.

The categories jump around chronologically, because the chronicler finishes up with Leah, before backing up to list the sons of the other women. But the sons of each woman are named in the correct birth order. This is the consistent method of the document, and it carries on that way without exception throughout chapter 2, listing the sons of Judah: Er, Onan, and Shelah, in that order. The sons of Tamar, Pharez and Zerah, are listed in that order. (even though in the birth account Zerah stuck his arm out first, but then drew it back, making Pharez the true firstborn Gen. 38:29) There is no instance of any son being named out of birth order. Then we come to chapter 3, where the family of David is named.

The first six wives of David are named, each bearing one son. That list is as follows:

1. Amnon- of wife Ahinoam
2. Daniel- of wife Abigail
3. Absalom-of wife Maachah
4. Adonijah-of wife Haggith
5. Shephatiah- of wife Abital
6. Ithream- of wife Eglah

Then the 7th wife, Bathsheba is named, and her four sons are named in the following order: Shimea, Shobab, Nathan, and Solomon. If the Chronicler is being consistent with his method, this makes Solomon the 4th son of Bahsheba, and also 10th son of the 7th wife of David. (Two numbers which have interesting typological value. Solomon being fourth in the birth order also likens him to Judah, the progenitor of the line, who was fourth born of Jacob.)
We suggest it is well established by all that has been recorded in the book of Chronicles to this point that if Solomon is named 4th, it places Solomon 4th in the birth order. If the chronicler is suddenly breaking with his method and mixing up the birth order to name the first-born 4th, it is very difficult to imagine any sensible rationale for doing so. By the time this genealogy was assembled,* Solomon was a towering historical figure, and the other sons of Bathsheba virtually unknown.

What reason can be imagined for a Chronicler to break from his consistent pattern and place Solomon 4th in the list, if he were not the 4th born? If the Chronicler were ordering the names according to prominence, or accomplishment, Solomon would clearly be named first. But he places Solomon 4th against all of that weight. For Solomon to be firstborn but placed fourth would be a highly unexpected oddity that cries out for an explanation.

In my view, the language of the narrative in another place, which is demonstrably summarizing and skipping ahead to certain selected points in the story, does not supply the needed explanation. In fact, it supplies no explanation. However, if Solomon is truly the 4th born, this is yet another instance of a well established Bible pattern: the younger surpassing the older. (Abel surpassing Cain,

Jacob surpassing Esau, Joseph surpassing his brothers, and David, the youngest of his brothers surpassing them all.)

*The names in the genealogy of Solomon that follows in the rest of chapter three extend for hundreds of years, into the Babylonian Captivity and out again in the time of Ezra. (Ch. 3:10-24) Ezra is often named as the author of the Bible's Chronicles.

² Endnote 2, page 20, Caleb a Gentile

The central thrust of *Solomon's Bride* is organized around overarching Bible themes. But occasionally, an exact scriptural point is made, such as this declaration by Solomon that Caleb is a gentile. I do not claim to have settled this question beyond all doubt, but can offer a case for it from the scriptures.

The case for Caleb being an Israelite is quite simple: Caleb was chosen as the leading representative of the tribe of Judah, when each of the tribes sent a spy into the Promised Land. (Numbers 13:6) Why on earth would they send a Gentile? This is a strong point, and I would not even consider another possibility without abundant scriptural evidence. I believe this evidence exists, and I will attempt to detail it here.

Firstly, Caleb's father Jephunneh is clearly called a Kenezzite, in four places, Numbers 32:32, and Joshua 14:6,13,14. This is unusual language to use of an Israelite. I can find no other case where the Bible goes out of its way to call an "Israelite" some other kind of "—ite." Uriah, *the Hittite*, is an example of the point: his being Hittite meant he was NOT Israelite. (2 Sam. 11:3) When the Bible does this, it is making the point that this person is NOT an Israelite. So now we have some dissonance, one strong Bible point rubbing against another. There has to be a truth to the matter. Let's look further, who are these "Kenezites?" According to Gen. 15:19, they are a *non-Israelite* tribe.

In the same day the LORD made a covenant with Abram, saying, Unto thy seed have I given this land, from the river of Egypt unto the great river, the river Euphrates: The Kenites, and the Kenizzites, and the Kadmonites, (Genesis 15:18, 19, KJV). (the underlying spelling, Kenezite and Kenizzite, is the same)

Not only were the Kenezites not Israelites, they were listed among the peoples that Abraham's children were to destroy. They were non-Israelite in the extreme. In other words, when Caleb's father is called a Kenezite, it is almost an insult! This demands our attention. If it were a neutral name, we might perhaps pass it by as an unexplained curiosity. But the Bible doesn't waste language. What point is the Bible making here in reminding us that Caleb is of a family over which hovered the curse of destruction?

Now, let's look at the name "Caleb." Ostensibly his parents named him that. But "Caleb" means, literally, "dog." It is the exact same word, the exact same spelling. In Gentile tradition, dogs were considered powerful and fierce. To name your son "dog" might be a complimentary choice in those circles. But for an Israelite to be named "dog" would again, be an insult. "Dog" meant, "heathen" or "Godless." Isn't that an extremely strange name for an Israelite father to give his son?

So, all these facts are tending toward a non-Israelite birth for Caleb. If that is true, there is a beautiful little jewel hidden here. Caleb was part of the "mixed multitude" that came out of Egypt, but so distinguished himself among Israelites that he was elected the representative of Judah, and given an inheritance "among" Judah, as the bible says. (not "in" Judah) *"And unto Caleb the son of Jephunneh he gave a part among the children of Judah..."*(Joshua 15:13, KJV). Similar language is used of Moses' Midianite father-in-law, Jethro. "And the children of the Kenite, Moses' father in law, went up out of the city of palm trees **with the children of Judah** into the wilderness of Judah, which lieth in the south of Arad; and they went and dwelt **among the people**."

This is as far as my understanding went when I was writing *Solomon's Bride*, and it was intriguing enough for me to include the possibility in the story. But upon examining the question further, I found more evidence in an unexpected place, the genealogy of Judah in 1 Chronicles 4. In this genealogy there appears the standard formula of father/son/father/son. This is true until you get to Jephunneh the father of Caleb, in verse 15. . . *and no father is listed!* Is this an "oversight," a scribal error? Or, is it a truth that connects with all the hints given above? Jephunneh is just dropped into the lineage of Judah . . . out of nowhere—no father in the line.* So how does his name get inserted there? Well, my best conclusion is, he is a gentile who is "grafted in."

Later in the *Solomon's Bride* story the point is made that in the Bible, a genealogy takes precedence over a narrative when it comes to determining lineage. This is because the Bible narratives have several purposes, historical, homiletical, etc. But a genealogy has ONE overriding purpose, to show for sure who is the father of who. As such, a genealogy could be set forth as proof of sonship/parentage in a legal proceeding where there is a dispute over an inheritance. When Cain is omitted from Adam's line, it is not an oversight, it means Cain is NOT Adam's son. And when Jephunnah has no father listed in the line of Judah, it means he was NOT born in that line. Somehow he is *grafted* in, fully adopted into the family of Israel, assuming full inheritance rights.

Something similar occasionally happened according to the Law under certain conditions. If a man had only daughters and no son, when the daughter(s) married, the son-in-law(s) would assume the inheritance. In the record keeping that followed, the son-in-law's name would appear in the genealogy to show the path of the inheritance. (The husband would have to be Israelite, of course) That is the only way according to the Law that I know of for a non-blood son to be adopted into an inheritance genealogy. But of Jephunneh, no such notation is made, and he was actually taken into the line of Judah *before* this Law came into effect. This statute was actually unknown to the Law until the four daughters of Zelophehad appealed to Moses on the basis that their father had no son. (Numbers 27:1-7) An exception was written into the Law based on that case, which demonstrates this had not been a standard understanding prior to the giving of the Law, as some other things had, such as burnt offerings, (offered by Abraham) clean and unclean animals, (chosen by Noah) etc. So, he cannot have gotten into the lineage by that route either. Therefore Jephunneh got into the line of Judah by some unknown rule, a "mystery," as such things are called in the New Testament. And if he was a gentile to begin with, not only did he get into the line of Judah, he got into the family of Israel from gentile origins.

This actually resonates typologically in the New Testament, because Caleb then becomes a type of all the gentiles who are grafted into Israel through Jesus Christ, (who is from of Judah according to the flesh) to take a share of the inheritance of Christ. (Romans

11:17)

To me, this is a strong collection of evidence, strong enough to overturn our unexamined assumption that the tribe of Judah would only appoint one born of that tribe as their representative. The point the Bible is making is, Caleb WAS fully Israelite, just not by birth. Under this arrangement, Caleb was fully of that tribe, enjoying all of its rights and privileges, and was therefore qualified to represent the tribe in every way. Yet he was born outside of it.

* I know of one other place where a name is inserted into a line without a listed father, and that is Seir, into the line of Esau, in 1 Chronicles 1:38. This is instructive in several ways. Firstly, we learn from comparison to the Genesis account that Seir's son Lotan had a daughter named Timna, who became Esau's son Eliphaz's concubine, who then became the father of Amalek! (See 1 Chronicles 1:39, Gen. 36:12) This was enough of a connection between the line of Seir and Esau for the chronicler to list all seven of Seir's sons in Esau's line. (1 Chronicles 1:38) This merging of the two lines later became so complete that "Mt. Seir" and "Esau" were almost Bible synonyms. The Chronicler inserts this connection in the genealogy to show how the merging of Esau and Amalek first happened. This instructs us that the Chronicler does not insert a name into a line accidentally, or for random purposes. In this case the purpose is uncovered by comparing the genealogy to details in other scriptures.

³ Footnote 3, page 34, Jephthah and his daughter

When I first drafted this chapter, I was informed by reviewers that there is a less violent interpretation of what happened between Jephthah and his daughter. Jephthah's vow reads like this: *And Jephthah vowed a vow unto the LORD, and said, If thou shalt without fail deliver the children of Ammon into mine hands, Then it shall be, that whatsoever cometh forth of the doors of my house to meet me, when I return in peace from the children of Ammon, shall surely be the LORD'S, and I will offer it up for a burnt offering.* (Judges 11:30, 31, KJV).

From this passage it seems clear enough that his daughter, being the unfortunate comer at the wrong moment, was to be sacrificed. The other proposed interpretation is, the daughter was sacrificed to the LORD in a *marital* sense, that is, she would be consecrated to God sort of as a Nun, and her father would never give her in marriage. I had heard this interpretation before, and it derives from this statement from Jephthah's daughter at the end of the account:

And she said unto her father, Let this thing be done for me: let me alone two months, that I may go up and down upon the mountains, and bewail my virginity, I and my fellows. And he said, Go. And he sent her away for two months: and she went with her companions, and bewailed her virginity upon the mountains. And it came to pass at the end of two months, that she returned unto her father, who did with her according to his vow which he had vowed: and she knew no man. (Judges 11:37-39, KJV).

That "she knew no man." and "bewailed her virginity" is given as the evidence that her life was not offered as an actual human sacrifice, just her future as a married woman. Either way it happened is not critical to the Solomon's Bride story, for Naamah is harboring many errors of fact. She could have been told this daughter was sacrificed, even if she was not. So I dismissed the question, and picked one of the two options. Since that time, the option I chose has been troubling to some readers, to a degree that caused me to re-examine the question.

In my original thinking, I found the daughter's bewailing of her virginity intriguing, but not compelling enough to overturn Jephthah's crisp vow, "(it)...*shall surely be the LORD'S, and I will offer it up for a burnt offering."* Nowhere else in the scripture does a "burnt offering" mean anything other than an actual sacrifice, and the account concludes that he *"did with her according to his vow."* His vow was a burnt offering. The body of the animal "burns" on the altar before the Lord. It's hard to get around that. So, *of course* she was bewailing her virginity, for she would not *live* to marry! Also, the idea of a sort of "nuns existence" for maidens dedicated to service of the Lord is completely foreign to anything found in the Laws of Moses. In all Israelite worship, the officiating was performed by the high priests from the family of Aaron, and the related work performed by the Levites ordained for that job. All were men, there were no ritually consecrated women prescribed anywhere in the Law. So we would have to inject into scripture two things that appear nowhere else, to take this interpretation.

But since that time, I have become aware of two more things that make the less violent possibility more likely. Firstly, Jephthah's vow may not be as crisp as it sounds, for the "and" could be translated "or." (The Hebrew conjunction, which is a "vav" prefixed to the word, is somewhat generic) Rendered this way, it would read, "(it) *shall surely be the LORD'S, -OR- I will offer it up for a burnt offering.*" Read this way, Jephthah was foreseeing that it might be either a person or an animal that would come forth from the "doors of (his) house." Grammatically, it does seem to be a valid possibility, and since we have hints of another meaning from his daughter's statements at the end of the story, worthy of consideration. (Why he would imagine an animal would come out of his house is still a bit of a question to me.)

In any case, all of this assumes that Jephthah had a rather loose understanding of the Law of Moses, to even be thinking this way. And if he was that confused, he could have been also confused about the role of men and women in the Levitical worship rites. That he blurted out in vow something he so regretted later is instructive, and raises the question, just how far could his ignorance extend? Jephthah had, prior to this event, been banished from living with his family, because he was the son of an harlot. (Judges 11:1) According to Levitical law, that disqualified him and his line from fellowship for ten generations. (Deuteronomy 23:2) He was *recruited* to come back and fight against the Ammonites, and he accepted on the condition that he would be accepted back into the family. (which they agreed to) So, he had been living among pagans for some time, and even the Israelites in his family back home were loose about what could be permitted by the Law. Under these conditions, *anything* is possible. Which brings to bear the second point:

At this time in Israelite history, the Canaanites religions had made very serious inroads into Israelite life. The Israelites had served those gods, there were no prophets to bring a clear word, and understanding of the Law of Moses was muddled and mixed. Ugaritic literature proves that Canaanites worship had no hesitation to the participation of women, they were priestesses, high priestesses, temple prostitutes, and doubtless had other roles as well. It could be that Jephthah had experienced the Law of Moses in a less than pure form, with ideas from other religions mixed in. (Just as the Roman Catholic church today practices many of the rites of the Roman pagan religion under Christian paint) That he could be confused enough to offer his daughter as a "consecrated priestess," is well within the realm of possibility. The problem is, he could then also be confused enough to offer her as a burnt offering, for the Canaanites did that too!

So, with this re-examination of the scriptures, and the careful consideration of what kind and learned readers have sent in, I conclude— I honestly don't know. It is not critical to me either way, nor is it critical to the Solomon's Bride story. So I leave the story as is, and add this footnote for the benefit of those readers for whom this is an important question. My dear precious reader, you may be right!

Made in the USA
Coppell, TX
28 November 2021

66601324R00121